"You've already become a hero around here anyway."

"How's that?" Matt met Shay's gaze.

"Word gets out. By now everyone knows of your work at the clinic. I bet they can all tell you about what happened with Mr. Clayton."

His eyes narrowed. "How would they know that?"

"One of Ms. Gladys's nephews works at the hospital. I'm sure one of the nurses has reported back."

"Oh." He glanced toward Ms. Gladys's again. "Anyway, thanks for the lawn mower instructions and not making fun of me more than you did."

She smiled. "Not a problem. I'm glad I could help. I hope your self-esteem is still intact."

"It has been shaken, but I think I will recover."

Shay grinned. "If you get really good at mowing and you like doing it, you can always cut Ms. Gladys's and Ms. Adriana's yards as well as the other neighbors'. They'll love you forever. That'll help rebuild your ego."

After the beating it had taken over the years, he could use some of that admiration. What would it be like to have a close relationship with his neighbors? With Shay?

Dear Reader,

This has been an interesting time in our lives and getting to escape into a world of excitement and love is refreshing. That's what happened for me while writing this book. I got caught up in the story and forgot the world around me. I hope it has the same effect on you.

Sometimes a story comes along that just surprises me. This is one of them. I got the seed of the idea from a TV show and ran with it. As I explored Matt and Shay's story, I became good friends with them and learned to appreciate the people they are. I was excited they found their happily-ever-after. I hope you enjoy it, as well.

As always, I love to hear from my readers. You can contact me at www.susancarlisle.com.

Happy reading!

Susan

TAMING THE HOT-SHOT DOC

———

SUSAN CARLISLE

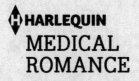

HARLEQUIN
MEDICAL
ROMANCE

HARLEQUIN®
MEDICAL
ROMANCE™

Recycling programs
for this product may
not exist in your area.

ISBN-13: 978-1-335-40872-3

Taming the Hot-Shot Doc

Copyright © 2021 by Susan Carlisle

All rights reserved. No part of this book may be used or reproduced in
any manner whatsoever without written permission except in the case of
brief quotations embodied in critical articles and reviews.

This is a work of fiction. Names, characters, places and incidents
are either the product of the author's imagination or are used fictitiously.
Any resemblance to actual persons, living or dead, businesses,
companies, events or locales is entirely coincidental.

This edition published by arrangement with Harlequin Books S.A.

For questions and comments about the quality of this book,
please contact us at CustomerService@Harlequin.com.

Harlequin Enterprises ULC
22 Adelaide St. West, 40th Floor
Toronto, Ontario M5H 4E3, Canada
www.Harlequin.com

Printed in U.S.A.

Susan Carlisle's love affair with books began when she made a bad grade in mathematics. Not allowed to watch TV until the grade had improved, she filled her time with books. Turning her love of reading into a love for writing romance, she pens hot medicals. She loves castles, traveling, afternoon tea, reading voraciously and hearing from her readers. Join her newsletter at susancarlisle.com.

Books by Susan Carlisle

Harlequin Medical Romance

Miracles in the Making
The Neonatal Doc's Baby Surprise

First Response
Firefighter's Unexpected Fling

Pups that Make Miracles
Highland Doc's Christmas Rescue

A Daddy Sent by Santa
Nurse to Forever Mom
The Sheikh Doc's Marriage Bargain
Pacific Paradise, Second Chance
The Single Dad's Holiday Wish
Reunited with Her Daredevil Doc

Visit the Author Profile page
at Harlequin.com for more titles.

To Debbie.

Thanks for your friendship and support.

CHAPTER ONE

DR. SHAY LUNSFORD hurried up the short hallway to answer the insistent rapping on the front door of the Delta Medical Clinic. Would she have an emergency to deal with first thing in the morning? The clinic didn't open for another twenty minutes. She looked through the full glass door of what had once been a dress store in a strip mall.

A man with dark hair styled in the latest cut and sporting a closely clipped beard on his square jaw stood there. Surrounded by all that shading was a beautiful full mouth. Her attention drifted to his green eyes watching her so intently.

"We're not open yet." Shay would've said she knew everyone in Lewisville, a suburb of Jackson, Mississippi, but she'd never seen this man before. She would've remembered him. That mouth.

"I'm Dr. Matt Chapman. Didn't Dr. Warren tell you I was coming?"

Huh? What was the name of the doctor her Uncle Henry had called to say was on his way to help her? This guy must be him. He'd give her a few weeks of assistance until she found more permanent help. Her clinic had grown so fast in the last eight months she couldn't handle it on her own any longer.

She'd been in the middle of stitches on a man's hand when the receptionist, Sheree, had told her to expect new help on Monday. With a nod, Shay had continued her work and forgotten the details, like his name. She studied the guy before her. "Can I see some identification?"

The man's movie star mouth thinned into a line as he dug into the back pocket of his well-worn jeans. She watched as he pulled a square out of his wallet. With the card facing her, he plastered it between the glass door and the palm of his hand.

It was a California driver's license. He was one of the few people who could take a good license picture. She met his look, turned the lock and opened the door. "Okay. Come in."

As he moved past her, he smelled of lemony aftershave. Everything about him made him stand out from the average men in the area. His shirt appeared carefully pressed and his khaki pants were a brand that she recognized as one of the best. The brown shiny loafers on his feet screamed they cost money.

He shoved his wallet into his back pocket and murmured, "I'm not used to being carded to get into a public medical clinic."

She flipped the lock closed again. "We have to be careful here. We keep drugs that some people would break in to get."

He pursed his lips and nodded. "So, I look like a drug addict? Good to know."

Shay shook her head. "That's not what I meant."

That put a slight smile on his lips.

"I'm cautious when I'm here by myself. I worked too hard to get this clinic up and running to have it fail because I wasn't careful. Let's start again." She extended her hand. "I'm Shay Lunsford. You'll be helping me for the next six weeks."

The doctor took her hand, dwarfing it inside his larger one. He shook with a firm and confident grip with a nominal amount of movement and time. Is that how he would handle patients? Short and sweet? She hoped not. Could a simple handshake tell her that much about someone? If so, what had hers said?

Relieved to have her hand returned to her, she said, "I appreciate you coming. I can use your help. Our patients will start lining up in a few minutes. I'm gonna warn you, you won't get much downtime."

"That's the way I like it."

She chuckled. "Says a man who's never worked at the Delta Clinic before. Come on, I'll give you the ten-cent tour before we open the doors." She started down the hall. "Obviously, this is Reception and Waiting." She waved a hand around them at the tiny space with only six chairs. "Most of the waiting is done outside. We hope to one day find a larger space, but that's not happening anytime soon."

Shay continued on, warming to her subject. The clinic wasn't much to look at, but she was proud of it. Having it had saved her sanity after her marriage and husband died. "The clinic is associated with Jackson Medical Hospital. We get everything including trauma cases. The nurses are from the hospital and rotate in and out by the week. They're a good group. This is a patient-centered clinic and I treat them like family. I expect my staff to do the same. We do have a regular receptionist. Her name is Sheree Boyd. She should be here in a few minutes."

She glanced at Dr. Chapman. He looked around with interest. Shay continued, "We have six exam rooms, three on each side. And this one—" she pointed to the last one on the left "—we use for trauma cases.

"Here's our supply room and drug cabinet. You and I'll be the only ones with keys. The next room is our office. We have to share. Actually, it's more of a room with a table and two chairs. There's also a small bathroom with a shower off it."

"Noted."

She continued down the hall. "The last room's our break room slash storage space or whatever else we need."

He nodded. "Got it."

There was a knock at the back door ahead of her.

"That'll be Sheree." Shay walked to it and looked through the eyehole before opening the door to the woman with dark hair and skin. "Good morning."

"Hey, sweetie. They're already lining up outside." Sheree stopped in midstride and gave the new doctor a long look. "And who do we have here?"

"This is Dr. Matt Chapman. He's our help for the next few weeks."

Dr. Chapman offered his hand. "Nice to meet you."

"You too. I think you're not from around here with that Mister *GQ* look about you."

He shrugged. "I've been living in Los Angeles."

Sheree continued with a grin, "You do have the look of a movie star. I'm glad you're here." She directed a thumb toward Shay. "This girl has been working herself to death. She needs some time for a social life."

And there came the age-old argument between her and Sheree. Why didn't Shay go out more? "Okay, Sheree." Shay gave the words a sharp note. "When you're ready we'll take the first patients." She looked at Dr. Chapman. His focus remained on her as if she were a virus under a microscope. She swallowed hard. "Your exam rooms are on the left-hand side. If you have any questions just ask."

Matt shook his head. Coming to Lewisville, Mississippi, and working in a small clinic was like stepping into a surreal world he had no idea existed. Where he had been used to a modern glass-and-chrome hospital, he now walked out of a tiny examination room created by plaster walls in a space that had once been a business.

He looked down at the chart of his next patient. Before arriving here he'd seen one or two patients a day as an orthopedic surgeon, and most of that time they had been asleep. He'd now made a complete turnaround in the way he spent his day. Just this morning he'd seen fifteen patients so far. Yep, he had made a drastic change. Not one he'd anticipated but one he had to accept. He'd done the right thing by standing up for a patient even if the repercussions hadn't been what he'd expected.

He glanced toward the waiting room and out the large picture windows along the front of the clinic. He saw a line just as Dr. Lunsford said he would. Apparently, she hadn't been exaggerating about the number of patients the clinic saw.

Over the next few hours, he cared for people who had coughs, an infected toe, a boil—and the list of everyday complaints went on. The sort of issues he'd not seen since medical school. Here he was out of his treatment element as well.

Working at the clinic appeared nothing like the high-pressure, trying-to-get-ahead world he'd just left. He'd have to downshift some to fit in here. It was just as well he wouldn't be staying long. Being used to an adrenaline rush at least once a day, he would soon miss it. At least he had an exciting job waiting for him in Chicago.

But hadn't that fast pace been part of why he had to make a change from a job where he was becoming the bright and shining star to one of starting over? He'd questioned one of the senior surgeons' decisions in the OR and that had been the end of it. In Chicago, he would have his chance again. The surgeon in LA's influence didn't stretch all the way across the country, thank goodness. In Chicago Matt could regain what he'd lost.

He passed Shay Lunsford between exam rooms and she smiled at him. "How's it going?"

"So far so good." She had a nice smile. One that showed in her eyes. It made her go from attractive to pretty. She'd pulled her dark hair up on her head, and it was long enough it fell to her shoulders. Wearing a knit shirt and jeans, she looked more like a college student than a doctor responsible for a bustling clinic. She came up to his chest in height but the authoritative air around her suggested she stood much taller.

"Good to hear. Let me know if you have an issue." She knocked on an exam room door and entered.

As he continued to work through his patient list, his nurse, who had arrived while Shay had been showing him around, kept the rooms on his side of the hall filled.

The next time he passed the doctor he asked, "Is every day like this?"

She grinned, her eyes twinkling as she headed up the hall with the words flowing over her shoulder. "I thought you were used to busy?"

At noon the clinic doors closed for a thirty-minute lunch. Matt followed his nurse to the back room and took a seat at the table. He had to admit he'd worked every bit as hard here as he had in Los Angeles. The cases were just different.

The others had brought their lunches and started unpacking them.

Shay took the only empty seat, the one beside him. She sighed. "You weren't told to bring your lunch?"

He received only the basics when Dr. Warren had called and told Matt that his grand-niece could use his help while he waited to start his new position. As his mentor in medical school Matt felt he owed the man. The old doctor had express mailed Matt keys and directions to his boyhood home for Matt to live in while working in Lewisville. "Nope. I thought there might be a restaurant or drive-thru nearby. I can see I misjudged that."

"Don't worry about it. We'll share." Each of the women pushed something from their lunch toward him. Shay offered half of her sandwich.

Sheree chuckled. "We can't have the new doctor going hungry."

Hungry and not wishing to embarrass himself, he accepted the sandwich and bit into it. "I'll return the favor sometime. Maybe order pizza."

"Don't worry about it. We're just glad to have your help. How did it go?" Sheree tore open a package of cheese.

"Pretty good. Nothing I couldn't handle. Thanks to Marie." He nodded at the young dark-eyed nurse who'd assisted him. "I was able to find supplies without looking like I didn't know what was going on."

"This was a good day for you to start on, it's been fairly slow." Shay took a sip from her drink can.

"What do things look like when they get faster?" He took a bite of sandwich. It wasn't his usual lunch fare, but he was glad to have it. He liked to order from a gourmet café.

All the women laughed.

Shay said, "We can have almost twice as many. If we have a major case, then it can cause a backup to deal with."

He nodded. "Good to know."

Sheree pinned him with a look. "So, what brings you to Lewisville?"

He shrugged. "I'm just here to help out for a few weeks. I'm on my way to a position in Chicago."

All the women's attention remained on him.

Matt continued. "I'm an orthopedic surgeon. I'm between jobs for a few weeks and Shay's uncle knew she could use some help. He asked me and I agreed."

"That your Uncle Henry? The one who's the professor up north somewhere?" Sheree asked Shay.

"Yeah. He checks in a couple of times a month. During one of his calls, I told him how busy we were." She turned to him. "I have to admit I'm glad he sent you our direction."

Matt nodded. "Glad I could help." He looked at Sheree. "Dr. Warren was one of my professors at Northwestern."

Sheree's eyes widened. "I get it now. Small world."

As quickly as the group had sat down for lunch, they all cleaned up and returned to work. Shay didn't linger either.

So far Shay had been pleased with how well the fill-in doctor had worked out. She'd had her doubts at first, but she found Matt efficient and intelligent. Even better than those traits, the patients seemed to like him. She'd also heard no complaints from her staff. He and Sheree had quickly bonded.

The afternoon had been running smoothly until Sheree hurried down the hall toward Shay. "We have an emergency."

Behind Sheree came Mrs. Clayton supporting her husband as he held one of his hands wrapped in a bloody shirt.

"Bring him back here." Shay moved to the door of the trauma room.

The couple had just entered the door when Matt stepped out of an examination room. He glanced at the blood drops on the floor.

"Dr. Chapman, I may need your assistance." Shay followed the couple into the room.

"Sure. Right behind you."

Shay helped Mrs. Clayton to seat her husband on the exam table. "Tell me what happened, Mr. Clayton."

"I was working on the car and got my hand caught in one of the belts. I didn't pull it back fast enough."

In a gentle voice Matt said, "You'll be fine. We'll take good care of you."

Shay glanced at him where he stood beside her. "This is Dr. Chapman. He'll be helping me take care of you."

Mr. Clayton gave Matt a suspicious look before he turned white and his eyes rolled back in his head.

"Lay him down before he passes out," Matt said as he placed a hand on the man's back and lowered him to the table.

"Rachel, we need a blanket here and to treat for shock." Shay pulled out the extension on the table, took the man's feet and laid them across it.

"Dr. Lunsford, do you mind?" Dr. Chapman nodded toward the man's hand. "I have experience here."

"I want Dr. Lunsford."

Shay placed a hand on Mr. Clayton's shoulder. "Dr. Chapman cares for this type of injury more often than I do. Trust me, he can help you."

"Jim, let him do what he knows best." Mrs. Clayton's eyes held tears.

To Dr. Chapman, Shay said, "Go ahead."

With gentle movements, Matt started unwrapping the dirty material covering the hand. He said to no one in particular, "I need a pan, saline. This needs to be cleaned so I can see the damage. Set up for an X-ray."

He had gone too far. "Dr. Chapman, may I speak to you."

"Right now?" His disbelief filled his voice.

"In the hall, please." She stepped outside and to her relief he followed.

The gloves on his hands came off with a pop then the trash can top dropped with a thump after he threw them in. He pulled the door closed behind him with more force than necessary.

Shay faced him. "We're to stop the bleeding and transport. The rest will be handled at the hospital."

Matt gave her a piercing look. "I know what I'm doing. This is my area of expertise. Let me save this man's hand. If he has to wait, he might lose the use of it."

Shay vacillated between agreeing and standing her ground.

"Trust me."

She huffed. "You better be as good as you think you are."

"I won't disappoint you." Without another word he returned to the room. Pulling on gloves again, he finished removing the wrapping and examined the hand.

Rachel had already laid a paper pad on the table beneath Mr. Clayton's hand.

Shay intended to take some control back in her own clinic. To Rachel, Shay said, "Hold the pan under his hand while I pour the sterile water over it."

Matt stood close, watching as if making sure she did it correctly.

Her chest tightened at the sight of the skin peeled back showing severed ligaments and broken bones. She compressed her lips to prevent the hiss from coming out.

Matt spoke to her with complete authority. "You should call the hospital now and tell them to have the ortho and vascular guys standing by. Mr. Clayton will need to go straight to surgery."

"They'll want to make that decision." It wasn't his place or hers to call the shots.

"You need to make them listen. If they don't, they'll have lost precious time. Even a chance to save the use of his hand. He needs to be started on IV antibiotics right away."

Shay glanced at Mrs. Clayton. A tear rolled down the woman's cheek. Matt and Shay didn't need to argue in front of her or their patient. Shay finished emptying the container over the hand. Matt picked up the hand to examine it more closely. He worked with focus and confidence. His were the actions of the practiced surgeon he said he was.

Shay spoke to Mrs. Clayton. "Is Mr. Clayton allergic to any medicines you know of?"

"No," the woman answered.

"I'll take care of the call and get the antibiotic." Shay exited the room. By the time she returned, Matt and Rachel had their heads together as he continued to clean the hand.

Shay went around to the other side of the table. Matt glanced at her. Her attention went to placing a needle in the man's arm and attaching a bag of glucose and adding the strong, broad-spectrum antibiotic through the fluid.

"I need the largest gauze pads available, a cloth and a large bag of ice."

"I'll take over." Shay took the pan from the nurse.

"When will the ambulance be here?" Matt asked.

"Thirty minutes at best." Her response came out as level as his tone.

"That's an hour round trip. That's not acceptable. One of us will have to meet them."

Her head jerked up. "What?"

His look locked on hers. "The latest studies show surgery done under a three-hour ischemic time have the best success."

She didn't blink. "Then I should go. I know the way."

"Agreed." His attention went to the supplies Rachel had placed on a metal instrument table she'd pulled over beside him. He picked up the gauze.

"I'll do that." Shay took the roll from him. She started wrapping Mr. Clayton's hand from the fingertips down.

"It doesn't need to be too tight." When she finished, Matt said, "We need to pour the water over it." She did so. "Then wrap it in the towel."

She took care of that.

"A plastic bag goes over the hand. Then tape it at the wrist. Rachel, we'll take that bag of ice." Matt placed the hand into the bag of ice.

Shay secured the bag.

"This is the best we can do here." Matt looked around briefly, appearing disappointed.

"I'll get my purse and let the hospital know

I'll be meeting the ambulance. We'll take him out the back door. Rachel, please ride with me. Mrs. Clayton, you can meet the ambulance at the hospital."

The nurse nodded.

Matt snapped off his gloves. "I'll see to things here."

Shay had no doubt he would. The mild-mannered guy had turned into superdoctor.

CHAPTER TWO

MATT HEARD SHAY'S voice in the hall. She'd
returned. She'd been gone a little over an
hour and a half. He hurried into the hall.
"How did it go?"

"Fine. I met the ambulance as planned."
She walked by him on her way to the office.
"It looks like we've a few more patients to
see."

Thankfully it was almost closing time and
the waiting room had open seats. He'd been
busy while she'd been gone. More questions
would have to wait. An hour later he'd seen
his last patient and joined Shay in the office
to tie up loose ends from the day.

When he entered, she stood and walked
around her side of the table, resting her butt
against the edge. "Close the door, please."

He did as she said. What was going on?
She stepped close to him and bit out, "Don't

you ever get high-handed with me again and take over one of my cases."

Matt looked behind him, questioning who she spoke to. "I'm sorry. I don't know what you're talking about."

"The high-handed way you handled Mr. Clayton's case. This is my clinic and we have agreements with the hospital and protocols."

His jaw hardened. Was she like the surgeon he'd dealt with in LA? He sure hoped not. "I did what needed to be done. Weren't you interested in the best care for Mr. Clayton?"

"Of course, I was! I am."

"Then I was the one who needed to take the lead on the case. It was as simple as that."

She pointed a finger at his chest. "Maybe so but that still doesn't give you the right to start ordering me around when we have a tough case."

He looked down at the slim finger pressed against him then into Shay's snapping blue eyes. His fingers gently pushed her hand away. The softness of it registered before his fingers slipped away from hers. "I don't like having people pointing fingers at me physically or figuratively."

Shay's eyes widened. Her jaw jutted out at a determined angle. "And I don't like people countermanding me in *my* clinic. No matter what they think they might know. We discuss things here, not order each other around. I have the final word—always."

Matt had to admire her directness. He couldn't remember the last time someone spoke to him that way. Used to running his operating room, he had a tendency to take control. "Agreed. I'm sorry. I'll do better in the future."

Someone knocked on the door.

Shay stepped back, putting space between them. She pushed at her hair and called, "Come in."

Sheree stuck her head though the opening. "Good work today, you guys. I'm out of here. See you in the morning."

"See you," Shay called.

"Thanks, Sheree." Matt moved around the table and slumped into a chair.

She sat back in the one she'd been in when he came in and studied her tablet.

When he'd seen the clinic, he'd questioned if they would be as up-to-date with technology as he'd been used to, but had soon been given a tablet for keeping up with patient charts. It cut down on the amount of paper pushing he'd be required to do. He wasn't very good at tedious chores. More than one time he'd heard complaints about his inability to keep his charting in order.

Shay started typing, seeming to take no notice of him. He went to work as well. Silence surrounded them except for taps on the screen.

"Matt?"

"Mmm?" He looked at her with a raised brow.

"Is there anything about any of the patients you saw today that I need to know?" She watched him.

"Not that I can think of." Was she being conscientious about her patients or did she question his thoroughness?

"Other than Mr. Clayton's case how did it go for you today?" She crossed her arms and leaned on the table. He liked having her full attention. Jenna, his ex-girlfriend, hadn't been able to give him that even when they had been on a date. Thinking back, she'd spent more time on her phone than she had talking to him. Why hadn't he recognized that? They had been two people caught up in their careers who complemented each other.

"Pretty well. I do have to admit I was busy."

"Yeah. It can get intense around here.

Today was about average." She swiped the page on the tablet.

"Then it'll be interesting to see what it's like on a busy day. I did need to ask you what I should do about referring a couple of the patients I saw to a specialist. One needs a general surgeon and another an orthopedist."

"Make a note of their names and I'll check their charts and take care of referrals first thing in the morning."

"I don't think you need to review my work." He pushed the paper he'd written the names on toward her.

"Maybe not, but the patients seen in this clinic are ultimately my responsibility."

Matt's mouth tightened. He generally ran his world. He wasn't used to other doctors or people questioning his decisions. The idea of someone monitoring his work made his skin prickle. He stood. Now he understood how Dr. Walters had felt when he'd questioned his decisions in the operating room, but in that case Matt had been right. Walters had been endangering the patient. In this one, Matt knew he had done the right thing for the patients, not trying to cut corners.

"I'd like to hear how Mr. Clayton's doing. Have you heard anything?"

"No, but I'll call." She pulled out her

phone. Seconds later she spoke to the hospital. When she ended the conversation she said to Matt, "He's still in the OR. Otherwise he's doing well."

"That's good to hear. Will you be calling to check in on him later this evening?"

"Of course." She sounded insulted he'd had to ask.

"Would you mind letting me know his status?"

She nodded. "I'll make sure you have an update."

Glad she seemed to have gotten over her anger with him, Matt said, "Great. Let me have your phone and I'll program in my number." His fingers touched hers as she handed him the small device.

She jerked back.

Had it been an overreaction to being touched in general or by him in particular? Matt entered his number and set the phone on the desk. "Why don't we call it a day? I think we've earned it."

She sighed. "It has been an adrenaline-driven one. I have a few notes to make, then I'll be ready to go."

He watched as she double-checked the front door had been locked and checked all the exam rooms on their way to the back door. Shay watched over the simple clinic like it was her baby. What would it be like to have someone care that much about him? His mother had, but his stepfather certainly hadn't. The hospital had sided with the wrong doctor because of Dr. Walters's status. His girlfriend hadn't cared enough about him to move with him even when he'd offered marriage. Such devotion eluded him.

In the parking lot behind the clinic she said, "I'll see you tomorrow."

"Okay."

"By the way, in the morning you can park in the back, knock on the door and I'll let you in."

He stopped on his way to his car. "What time do you usually get here?"

"Around seven. That gives me an hour before opening to take care of supplies, extra charting and referrals. Even a little cleaning sometimes."

"Then I'll see you at seven. I can help out with those." He normally arrived at the hospital at 6:00 a.m. Arriving at seven would feel like sleeping in to him.

"It's not necessary."

"Maybe not, but I'll be here anyway. You can use my help or not. After that lecture this morning you shouldn't be here by yourself."

"I'm used to being here by myself." Opening the door to the car, she looked at him.

"That doesn't sound like a safe plan."

She glanced at him. "Well, up until you no one's even noticed."

"They should have. I'll hang around out in my car, then, if you'd rather I not come in, but I'll still be here at seven. Good evening, Shay." He started toward his car again.

She smiled. "I was glad to have your help today, Matt. The EMTs were impressed with how Mr. Clayton's hand had been secured."

He returned her smile. "You're welcome."

"See you tomorrow." Shay gave him a slight wave and climbed into her family-size sedan.

Matt continued along the side of the building to his navy sports car. He waited until Shay turned into the road before following her into the traffic. He hadn't been sure what to expect at the Delta Clinic. The one thing he was confident about was he hadn't expected the dynamo that was Shay Lunsford.

His drive home was uneventful with the exception of one missed turn. He traveled through well-established neighborhoods past shopping areas into the Jackson University area where Dr. Warren owned a 1950s bungalow he usually rented to students. Thankfully, it had been available for Matt. With white clapboard siding, large shrubbery and a small front porch it looked much like the rest of the houses on the tree-lined street with sidewalks on both sides.

He pulled into the paved drive and climbed out. The older woman who lived next to him stood at the end of her drive talking to another woman about the same age. She waved at him. He gave her a fixed smile and quick wave, then hurried into the house. In the places he'd lived, people rarely paid any attention to the others living around them. For the last ten years he'd lived in transit communities. Neighbors who would be gone in three months to a year wouldn't have been worth the time to meet, even if he'd had the time to meet them."

Gladys—he believed she'd said that was her name—had already been over to introduce herself and had even brought him a pie. Never had he had a neighbor bake for him. She'd totally taken him off guard. She'd done much of the talking and had asked him a number of questions about himself. The type of interest she showed made him a little uncomfortable. He'd hurried her on her way with a thank-you. At first, he'd been unsure about eating anything someone he didn't know had prepared, but one bite of Gladys's apple pie and that concern had flown out the window.

After popping something in the microwave for dinner, he got a drink and settled in front of the TV. Watching television had been a change for him. He'd rarely turned it on prior to coming here. He sank into the recliner, exhausted and grateful that Warren's house included furnishings. In Chicago, Matt would have to hire someone to handle furnishing his apartment. Matt looked around the room with a sigh of acceptance. It was nice to live in a house instead of an apartment, even for a short time.

He'd finished his meal and was reading a medical journal when his phone rang. "Hello."

"Matt, it's Shay."

She had a nice voice. "Hey."

"Is this a bad time?"

"No, no. What's up?" He sat up in the chair.

"I was just calling to tell you that Mr. Clayton is out of the OR and in a room. The doctors believe he's going to get back the full use of his hand. They praised how you took care of it."

"You had a part in it as well."

She paused. "Thanks for pushing. If you hadn't insisted…"

"It was a good day's work for both of us."

"I'm glad you were there." She sounded as if she meant it.

Why did it matter to him so much to have her praise? "I'm glad I could help."

"See you in the morning, Matt." She hung up.

He wished they had talked longer. He would've enjoyed her company even if it was over the phone.

The next morning Shay turned into the parking lot and drove to the back of the building. As Matt had promised he waited in his car. She had to admit it was nice to have someone there when she entered and exited the building. Even though she knew most of the people that lived in the area it still bothered her to go into the clinic alone.

When her husband had been alive and left for his first deployment she hadn't been wild about staying by herself, but she'd learned to deal with it at home and thought she would at the clinic as well.

Shay smiled at Matt as she stepped out of the car. He walked toward her. "Good mornin'."

"Good morning." He offered her a slight lift of his mouth.

She couldn't get over how sensual his lips were. No man had the right to have such a sexy mouth. She'd felt nothing for a man for so long it made her wary of him noticing something so personal. She didn't make a habit of paying attention to a man on that level…but for some reason he drew her. She wanted to know more about him. That was a new sensation. Maybe it was just curiosity because he was a stranger. "Did you get some rest last night?"

"I did. Much-needed rest." He fell into step beside her as they walked to the door.

Shay chuckled. "You didn't find anything exciting to do?"

"Nope. Didn't even go looking for something."

That surprised her. Somehow, she'd gotten the impression he wasn't a homebody type.

The rest of the week continued much the same way. She had to admit she looked forward to finding him waiting for her each morning. It had been a long time since someone had shown that type of concern for her. She missed it. Best of all Matt worked every bit as hard as she did and to her even greater surprise hadn't questioned her authority since the first day.

Friday evening Shay started out of the clinic parking lot when she noticed Matt hadn't started his car yet. She waited, watching in the rearview mirror for him to back out of his parking space. Instead, he stepped out of the car shaking his head.

She reversed her car and rolled down the passenger-side window. "Need a ride?"

Matt shook his head with a look of disgust on his face. He slammed the car door closed. "Yeah, it looks like I do. As skilled as I might be as a doctor, I have zero mechanic skills."

"Can't be good at everything. Come on, I happen to know someone who has great mechanic skills."

He climbed into her passenger seat, making the space feel much smaller. "We'll stop by Ralph's and ask him to come tow it to his place. Ralph's is the local garage in town. He's actually very good."

"Ralph's it is. The car is brand-new. I don't know what could be wrong."

"It's nice. We don't see many of those around here." She drove out of the parking lot. His attention remained on the road as if it made him nervous being a passenger.

"Is your husband or boyfriend going to

say anything about you riding around with some man?"

"My husband died three years ago and there's no boyfriend."

"I'm sorry. About your husband, not the boyfriend. That didn't come out right."

Shay giggled. She rather liked Matt being flustered. It was nice to know he could be after seeing him always so sure of himself. "It's okay."

As they reached town, she pulled into the lot of an old gas station. Cars lined the area.

Shay got out of the car. "Ralph should be around here somewhere."

Matt joined her as she strolled through the wide and high roll door. Inside she called, "Ralph?"

"Yeah." The muffled sound came from the back of the building.

She followed it. "Ralph, where are you?"

"Shay, is that you?" came a gruff voice.

Matt shook his head. "Do you know everyone?"

She grinned and shrugged. "Around here? Mostly. That's what happens when you live in the same place all your life." She continued around a car until she could see legs sticking out from under it.

Ralph rolled out on a dolly he lay on and looked up at her. "Shay, girl, how're you doin'?"

"Great, Uncle Ralph."

"Uncle Ralph?" Matt murmured beside her.

Ralph scrambled to his feet, picking up a rag and wiping off his hands. He eyed Matt suspiciously, studying him closely. "And who is this? I hope he's better than that last guy."

"Uncle Ralph! This is Dr. Matt Chapman. Uncle Henry asked him to come help me out for a few weeks while I look for another doctor for the clinic. His car wouldn't start. It's parked at the clinic. Do you think you could go and check it out? Tow it in if you can't get it started."

"Sure thing. It'll be a couple of days before I could get to it if it needs a part."

Matt pulled a face.

Shay turned to him. "Don't worry, I'll pick you up and take you home each day."

Matt crammed his hands in his pockets. "That seems like a lot of trouble. I can just rent a car."

She briefly placed her hand on his arm. "I don't mind giving you a ride. It's the least I can do for a visitor."

"Thanks, I appreciate that. I hate to put you to so much trouble."

Shay smiled at him. "Hey, that's what we do around here. Help friends out."

A baffled look came over Matt's face before he fished around in his pocket for his keys. "I appreciate that."

"Thanks, Uncle Ralph."

"Sure, Shay, girl." He turned to Matt. "You better be nice to Shay. She's a special one."

Matt looked taken aback. "Uh…yeah, sure."

Shay colored pink with mortification. There was nothing like being overprotected. She'd lived through the humiliation of being the topic of conversation when the town had found out about what John had done. Over time it had turned to protecting her. They wouldn't let her be hurt by anyone again.

Back in her car, Shay turned out of the gas station and headed through town.

Matt looked back at the station with a perplexed frown. "What was that all about?"

"I'm sorry about that. It's old history. Nothing to do with you." He glanced at her. But thankfully he changed the subject.

"Where're we going?"

She glanced at him. "I'm taking you home."

His brows rose. "You didn't even ask me where I live."

Shay smirked. "I've been to Uncle Henry's hundreds of times."

"I forget you are family."

"How did the two of you become such good friends?" She shifted lanes and headed toward the university.

"I think he recognized someone eager to learn who needed a father figure."

What an odd statement. She looked at his profile for a moment before she had to turn her attention back to driving. Not sure how to respond, she said, "Uncle Henry is a nice guy."

"He made a real difference in my life. Still does."

Shay glanced at him. "How do you find living in Jackson?"

"I like it. I can get around much quicker than I'm used to. Or at least I could until my car wouldn't run. Less traffic I have to admit is nice. Even the pace at the clinic is slower, even though we stay busy. There's a different feel."

"It's nice to know we have some charms." She grinned.

"Charms. That's a nice way of putting it. I've lived all my life in one large city or another. I've never thought of them as having charms."

"Every place has good attributes and bad, I'd guess." She made a left turn.

He looked at her. "And what would you say Lewisville's attributes are?"

"Love and acceptance." She'd had them, then questioned if they were gone, to soon learn they had never left.

"That's nice." A sadness filled his voice.

Her eyes met his. Had he not had love and acceptance in his life? "I'll say that living in the same place from childhood means that people know more about you than you might want them to."

"I'm not sure I'd like that. It makes me uncomfortable to know people know where I live without me even telling them. Do you mind so many knowing your business?"

She'd lived the last few years feeling humiliated as the center of gossip. It wasn't until she'd started devoting her time and energy to building a clinic in the Lewisville area that she'd started hearing less about her past and more about the good she was doing. "It shows that the townsfolk of Lewisville care about each other."

"You didn't exactly answer the question

and I won't push. Even with the good and bad it's nice to know someone cares."

Had he felt unwanted in some place by someone?

A week later Matt looked out the car window as Shay made a right turn onto his street.

"Tell me, have a Ms. Gladys and Ms. Adriana been fighting over you?" she asked.

He'd had a few women aggressively come after him, but his seventy-something neighbors had taken it to a whole new level.

"I wouldn't exactly call it fighting over me, but I'll say I've got a freezer full of casseroles."

Shay chuckled. He liked the sound. "I'm not surprised. There's always been competition between the two of them. I think they've been competing for the same boys since they were in elementary school. Uncle Henry eats it up when he's home. Says it's good for a bachelor's soul to still have women after him."

"And here I was thinking I was special." He'd not always felt that way. Most of his life he'd worried if he had been good enough. Apparently, Jenna hadn't thought so. His stepfather had made him feel the same.

While Shay drove down the street, he studied all the well-kept yards. All of them looked neat and tidy except for his. He winced. He never before felt a need to keep up with his neighbors. But at this moment, shame filled him. Hell, he hadn't even known any of them before coming to Jackson.

"Apparently, we've been keeping you so busy you can't get your grass cut."

His chin lowered to his chest. "Something like that. In my defense it has been cut once since I moved in, but I didn't do it. I just came home, and it was done. No one left me a note or bill."

Shay laughed. "It's our way of saying welcome and also to remind you to take care of your yard."

"Sort of like a backhanded compliment."

"Something like that." She pulled into his drive. "Do you not have a lawnmower?"

He gave her a chagrined look, not meeting her eyes. "It's more like I've never mowed grass before. I don't know anything about a lawnmower."

She brought the car to a jerking stop and turned to look at him with her mouth open. "You've never mowed a yard?"

He winced. "I'm not sure whether I should be ashamed or glad, but no, I haven't."

Her eyes were wide with pure disbelief. "How's that possible?"

Both his brows rose. "If you pay to have it done, or don't have a yard."

"You've really lived a sheltered life." Shay shook her head. "I guess if you lived in an apartment all your life you could have never mowed grass, or if you were rich enough to pay someone. Which are you?"

"Mostly living in an apartment."

"Around here, we have to cut grass." She pulled farther up in the drive. "Would you like me to show you what to do?"

"I would be grateful. I think my neighbors would be as well." He should have been embarrassed, but for some reason he liked the idea of Shay showing him such a skill.

"Today, Dr. Chapman, you'll learn something new. You'll have an experience to talk about when you leave Lewisville." Pride and humor filled her words.

He studied her pert nose and sparkling eyes. Matt suspected he'd remember more than how to mow grass when he got to Chicago. "I guess I will."

She turned off the engine. "Where's the mower?"

"I saw one in the shed." He climbed out of the car.

Shay followed him to a small building behind the house. He opened the door and pulled out the push mower. She stepped up beside him like he had done during the emergency. Here she had far more confidence than he did.

"Pay close attention," she instructed. "I don't want you to miss anything, Doctor."

He moved in closer. "Shay, you're enjoying this far too much. I do have a fragile ego."

"I doubt that. I've just never known someone who has never mowed grass, not even once."

"I can't be that rare." His ego in some areas could be weaker than he might let on.

"Okay, now I may be making fun of you." A silly grin covered her mouth.

I'd like to kiss that grin. Wow. Those thoughts were better left alone. "Thank you for at least seeing it my way." He shoved his hands in his pockets.

Her look turned serious. "Let me start over. Would you like me to show you how to start the mower and how to use it?"

He looked around at the calf-high grass then at the other houses' yards. "Please. I think Ms. Gladys and Ms. Adriana would appreciate it if I learned."

Shay smiled before she turned back to the

machine. "Okay, the first thing we need to do is check to see if there's enough oil. You never want to run the engine without there being enough oil in it." She opened a little top and looked inside before closing it.

"Oil. Got it."

"Now we need to see if there's enough gas." Shay turned another top and checked inside. "There's plenty of gas." She looked around in the shed and pointed. "There's a can if you need more gas."

He cocked his head locating the red plastic can. "Okay."

"The next step is to start it. This can be tricky if it hasn't run in a while. Pump this." She pushed a button in three times. "This is the choke. Now pull this bar up and hold it. Then pull the cord." She reached over.

He stopped her and pulled the cord. The machine coughed. Matt let the cord go back in and pulled again. The mower roared to life. He stepped close to her and said into her ear, "I think I can take it from here."

Shay stiffened.

He held the bar down. Shay stepped away from him sweeping an arm out, indicating for him to go to it. He made one pass around the yard and came back to her.

As the mower rattled to a stop, he grinned. "Nothing to it."

"Says the man who didn't mow his grass 'cause he didn't know anything about a lawn-mower."

He nodded. "Point taken."

"I think you've got it from here, so I'd better go." She glanced at the house next door where the curtain had been pulled back and Ms. Gladys watched them. "You might get a cake out of this."

He gave the older woman a wave and the curtain dropped back. "I guess I'll be the talk of the street because you had to show me how to start the mower."

She placed a hand on his forearm. "You'll survive. You've already become a hero around here anyway."

"How's that?" Matt met her gaze.

"The word gets out. By now everyone knows of your work at the clinic. I bet they can all tell you about what happened with Mr. Clayton."

His eyes narrowed. "How would they know that?"

"One of Ms. Gladys's nephews works at the hospital. I'm sure one of the nurses has reported back."

"Oh." He glanced toward Ms. Gladys's

again. "Anyway, thanks for the lawnmower instructions and not making more fun of me than you did. I've rarely felt so inept in my life, but I did about the mower. I'm also indebted to you for taxiing me around. Hopefully your uncle Ralph will have my car done next week."

She smiled. "Not a problem. I'm glad I could help. I hope your self-esteem is still intact."

"It has been shaken but I think I will recover."

Shay grinned. "If you get really good at mowing and you like doing it you can always cut Ms. Gladys's and Ms. Adriana's yards as well as the other neighbors'. They'll love you forever. That'll help rebuild your ego."

After the beating it had taken over the years, he could use some of that admiration. What would it be like to have a close relationship with his neighbors? With Shay?

CHAPTER THREE

ON THURSDAY AFTERNOON of the next week, Shay stepped out of the examination room of the clinic in search of Matt. She could use his expertise with this case. Looking one way then the other, she spotted him at the reception desk talking to Sheree.

He must have sensed her need because he looked in her direction. As she started toward him his forehead wrinkled and his appearance darkened with concern. He spoke to Sheree and walked toward Shay. "What's wrong?"

"I'd like to get your opinion on a patient."

His shoulders eased. "Sure. What's the issue?"

"Joey is eight. He had a broken arm last year. Now he's complaining of aches and pains. I thought with your background you might have some ideas." Shay sure hoped so. She was out of them.

Matt's voice lowered. "Have you considered abuse?"

Shay shook her head. "I've known his mother, Beth, all my life. She would never abuse him."

"What about the father?"

Shay stiffened. "Him either. I don't want to go down that road until I have exhausted all other ideas. Something else has to be going on."

Matt gave her a firm look. "I have to warn you I will do what has to be done if I find out differently."

"You won't, but if abuse turns out to be the issue, I'll handle it. I know the law and my duty."

"Okay then, let's see the patient." He stepped back so she could open the door to the examination room.

Shay entered and Matt joined her, closing the door behind them.

"Beth, this is Dr. Chapman. He's an orthopedic surgeon."

Shay's petite blond friend quickly stood. "Surgeon? Joey doesn't need surgery, does he?"

Stepping forward, Shay laid a hand on Beth's arm. "No, Dr. Chapman's here helping me. He just happens to be an orthopedic doctor so I thought he might have some ideas about what's causing Joey's problem. There's nothing to worry about."

Matt moved to Joey, who sat on the examination table. "Hello, Joey. I'm Dr. Chapman and I'd like to have a look at you, would that be okay?"

The eyes of the boy with the white-blond hair widened as he gripped the edge of the table. He looked at his mother. Joey's fearful look eased as his mother sat down in the chair. "I guess so."

Shay watched as Matt bent his long frame until he came to eye level with the boy. "Can you show me where it hurts?"

"All over." The boy pointed to his thighs and arms.

"Not in any one spot?" Matt's voice remained even while his manner remained intent.

Joey shook his head.

"Good," Matt said with a nod. "I need to touch you. Will that be all right?"

Again, Joey nodded.

Matt proceeded to run his hand over the boy's legs from his feet upward. "I hear you broke your arm. What were you doing when that happened?"

"I fell while I was playing a baseball game."

Matt glanced back at Shay as if to say maybe she was right about there not being any abuse.

He continued to run his hand confidently over the boy's limbs. "What position do you play?"

"Shortstop," Joey said proudly.

"That's an important position."

Shay couldn't help but admire how Matt put the boy at ease. She'd overheard other patients when they were leaving the clinic talking about how much they had liked Matt. She could see why. He had a way with people.

"Joey, do you mind if we take some X-rays of your arms and legs? I know you must've had them done when you broke your arm. They don't hurt. The nurse will take you down the hall for the pictures while I talk to your mom for a minute."

Joey looked at his mother. She nodded and he slid off the exam table. He winced when his feet touched the floor.

Shay stepped to the door and opened it. Her nurse waited there. "Lucy, will you take Joey for X-rays of his legs and arms."

As they walked down the hall, Shay returned to Matt and Beth. The two women's attention focused on Matt. He leaned his hip against the examination table and faced them.

Shay swallowed, unsure she'd like what he had to say.

"I think Joey has what is called fibrous dysplasia. It's a rare disorder."

"Oh, my." Beth's hand covered her mouth.

Shay placed a hand on her friend's shoulder. Shay looked at Matt. "I thought it might be."

He gave her a wry smile and spoke to Beth. "We'll be able to confirm it with the X-rays. It can't be cured, but it can be controlled. Unfortunately, it'll require some surgery. Shay can give you the name of a doctor here in Jackson who can oversee Joey's case. Or if you wish, I'll be glad to—but you'd have to travel to Chicago."

Beth took a deep breath. "What do we need to do now?"

Shay stepped away from her. "Beth, why don't you take Joey out for an ice cream on me and I'll let you know what the X-rays show. You and Luke can talk about this. I can get names together for who to see. I'll see that Joey has the best care he can receive."

Matt stood. "And I'll do all I can to help as well."

Shay looked at him and mouthed *thank you*.

He nodded. "Then I'll go."

Shay watched him quietly slip out the door. She hated giving bad news but somehow it had been easier with Matt's support.

That evening, Matt rode home with Shay with a heavy heart.

"I checked the X-rays and I'm confident Joey has fibrous dysplasia. His bones look like ground glass. A sure sign. Let me know how I can help."

Shay looked over at him. "I'm just glad you were here to confirm what I suspected. You were really great with Joey. Especially for a surgeon."

A wrinkle formed on his forehead. "What exactly does that mean?"

"Surgeons aren't known for having great bedside manners since most of their patients are asleep."

"I think I've been offended. I have to meet with them before and after surgery. They're awake then. So, I do have some skills."

Shay grinned. "Touchy, are you?"

In that area of his life, he was. He'd worked so hard to make his stepfather proud of him and never felt he hit the mark. It was nice to hear he had done well in Shay's eyes. "Maybe, a little bit. I've not always been great with people."

"That's hard to believe. I've heard nothing but good things about your interactions with patients."

"That's good to know. It doesn't come natural." He'd too often let his feelings toward his stepfather bleed over into his interactions with people, fearing they would treat him the same as his stepfather did. Jenna had more than once accused him of closing himself off. Maybe he did.

Shay's phone rang. She punched her hands-free button and spoke into the speaker. "Hello."

"Hey, Shay. It's Billy. I'm not gonna be able to play in the game Sunday. Addison called to tell us she's on her way to the hospital to have the baby."

"Oh, wow. I understand, Billy. Give Addison my best. Be sure to send pictures. Don't worry about the game." She gave Matt a pointed look with a gleam in her eyes. "I'll find someone to replace you."

What were they talking about? Shay's look and her tone of voice didn't bode well for him. He'd seen it in other women's eyes when they wanted something.

With a slight lift to her lips Shay said, "I think I already found a replacement. You go on and give that new grandbaby a kiss from me."

"Thanks, Shay. I hate to miss one of the highlights of the year."

"There's always next year. Take care, Billy." Shay punched the button ending the conversation.

Shay didn't immediately say anything to him. The conversation hung between them. She was good, he'd give her that. His curiosity finally got the better of him. "What was that about?"

"I've got to find a replacement for Billy on my softball team." She continued to focus on the road.

"You play softball?" Matt shouldn't have been surprised, but she'd never mentioned it.

"Only once a year."

Matt turned so he could better see her. "That's interesting. Why once a year?"

"I organize a community game to raise money for the clinic. We play Sunday afternoon at two. Now we're short a team member. It'll be pretty hard for my team to win if I don't have enough players." She glanced at him.

"Why haven't you mentioned this game before?"

Shay shrugged. "I don't know. I figured you wouldn't be interested."

Her tone made him feel guilty. Of what he wasn't sure. He felt he should defend himself.

"Would you help me out and take Billy's place? Please."

His chin dropped and he narrowed his eyes. "Are you begging?"

"It's something I don't like to do, but in this case I'm desperate." Her tone sounded serious, but she grinned.

"*Desperate*. Interesting word." Matt pursed his lips and nodded. He had started to enjoy this. "So, I'm better than nothing."

"That's not exactly what I was saying."

He put a hurt tone in his voice. "Sure sounded like that to me."

She sighed. "Come on, Matt, will you help me out?"

He chuckled. "I'll do it."

A bright smile covered her face. "Great. Thank you so much. Have you ever played softball?"

Her obvious jab made him glad he'd agreed. "A couple of times, but I'm much better at baseball."

"Why am I not surprised? I think you'll have a good time."

He'd started to think he might enjoy anything he shared with Shay.

"I'll pick you up around one o'clock unless you'd like to go to church with me. We've a covered dish meal afterward, then we'll go to the ballpark for the game."

Overwhelmed, he wasn't sure he should sign on for all of that. "I don't know."

"Come on, Matt, live dangerously. You might be surprised." She grinned. "You afraid?"

He'd take her challenge. "Okay. What time should I be ready?"

"I'll pick you up at ten thirty."

As Shay drove away from his house Matt questioned if he was wading in too far. He liked being a part of this slower pace of life, but he shouldn't get used to it. Or being around the intriguing and full-of-surprises Shay.

Shay shifted closer to Matt to give Mr. and Mrs. Griffin room to join them on the church pew on Sunday morning. Having to sit pressed against Matt hadn't been in her plans. The church buzzed with talk of him attending with her. Maybe she'd gone too far by inviting him. Gossip had been what she'd been avoiding for the last few years. Not that she'd been able to after letting it be known that John had been planning to divorce her. Bringing a man to church with her would only start the tongues going again.

The side of Matt's solid, warm body pressed against her made her want to forget the fact that they were the topic of the day. She should have known better. It had been a long time since she'd been so close to a man. She glanced at Matt. He acted unaffected.

Grateful the service had begun and for having to stand to sing, which gave her space away from Matt, the distance didn't last long when he shifted to look over her shoulder to see the hymnal. As disconcerting as she found being near him there was something about it she found desirable, like having someone special in her life. A man who stood strong beside her.

Now her thoughts had turned to those of a sad widow woman desperate for attention, interested in the first handsome man who came along. He hadn't even shown any real interest in her and here she sat daydreaming of would-haves and could-haves.

Even if he was interested, what could they have but a fling? Matt had no plans to stay in Lewisville. His destiny was Chicago. She never planned to move. This was her home, where she belonged. But how many times would someone like Matt come along? For once in a long while she felt alive again.

She had no idea of what the sermon was about. Her head remained full of Matt and what-ifs. She moved as far as she could away from him, but when she did, he swallowed up the space with his leg coming to rest against hers once more. He appeared to be contently listening with no idea of the conflict he created in her. Not soon enough for her the service came to a close.

Matt let her step out into the aisle in front of him when the service was over. They were immediately stopped by Mrs. Lyles.

"Shay, I haven't met your visitor." The woman who had taught Shay in grade school studied Matt.

"Mrs. Lyles, this is Dr. Matt Chapman. He's helping me at the clinic for a few weeks and playing in the softball game. Matt, this is Mrs. Lyles."

Matt gave the woman a warm smile. "It's nice to meet you."

"And you too." Mrs. Lyles smiled in return. "You know Shay is very special to us."

He looked at Shay with a raised brow then turned back to the woman. "I'm figuring that out."

Three more women came up behind Mrs. Lyles.

"We want to meet this handsome man," Mrs. Smith said.

"Yes. Is this the doctor we've been hearing all about?" another in the group asked.

Shay introduced the women to Matt, who suffered through the introductions with a polite smile on his lips, before they were interrupted by the pastor who introduced himself and engaged Matt in conversation.

Knowing she'd had enough of the inquisition and that Matt no doubt wanted to run, Shay took his arm at the first break they got and headed for the front door. She led him down the steps, not stopping until they were alone under a large oak tree. "I'm sorry about that."

"I haven't been to church in years," he said, sounding breathless and relieved. "I'd forgotten what it was like to be the new guy."

She chuckled. "It's a weekly occurrence without fail here. Sorry about the horde wanting to meet you."

"No problem. I guess it's better than no one noticing."

"I wouldn't know, but I think I might like experiencing that sometime." She looked around at people still mingling in front of the church.

"Are they always so…um…protective of you?"

"I'm sorry if they pried." It would be a long time before she brought another man to church with her. Even for an innocent reason.

"Hey, we're good. I think it's nice that you're so loved and appreciated. Nowhere have I lived that I've had that."

At one time she wouldn't have seen the close attention as welcome. She'd felt like a disappointment to them for so long. "Have you recovered enough to go under the microscope again?"

He rolled his shoulders. "I think I can handle it."

She grinned and tugged on his arm. "Then let's go get something to eat. I promise the food will be worth the pain."

They walked around the side of the white shiplap building with the high steeple.

Matt stopped. "Wow. This is amazing. I've heard of people doing this, but I've never seen anything like it."

Shay looked at the long tables set up end to end underneath the large open pole shed under the hundred-year-old oaks. Ladies worked like ants as they arranged food on one table while others brought it out from the back of the church. Other church members circled around waiting for them to finish their chores. More tables were covered in thin plastic tablecloths and had folding chairs beneath them waiting for hungry people who were already lining up to fill their plates.

Shay watched Matt. His eyes were wide and bright in anticipation. "Yeah, it's almost like you can hear the tables groaning in pain."

"I've never seen so much food in one place. And I've been to a number of fancy banquets." His awe hung in the air.

He'd just confirmed they were from two different worlds. The nicest event she'd attended had been her own wedding reception held inside the church. "All I can say is welcome to the South. Where we do believe in eating."

They moved over to where the line had formed and took their places. People continued to come up to speak to her, but they were really interested in Matt.

He whispered in her ear, "Does every new person in town get this kind of treatment?"

"They're just curious." She handed him a plate and grinned. "Enjoy filling it up."

Shay went down one side of the table while

Matt moved down the other. She glanced over to see the food piling up on his plate and smiled.

When he joined her at the end of the table, he looked at his plate. "I have no idea where I think I'm planning to put all this."

She chuckled. "You afraid your eyes are bigger than your stomach, Doc?"

"Yeah."

"And to think you haven't even seen the desserts yet."

He looked around as if searching for that table. "And sweets are my weakness."

"Come on, let's find you a place to sit down so you can get started on all that." Shay looked out over the sea of people. Her mom waved and pointed to two empty chairs across from her and Shay's father.

"Brace yourself, you're going to be eating with my parents."

He hesitated a moment. "I look forward to meeting them. Will they ask a lot of questions about why I'm with you?"

"Maybe. But I'll handle them."

He met her gaze. "I can take care of myself, Shay."

"Okay. Just don't say I didn't warn you."

They took their seats. Before she had a chance, Matt smiled at her parents and introduced himself. He skirted her mother's questions by digging into the food and making sounds as if he had found nirvana. Shay couldn't help but laugh.

"This has to be the best potato salad I've ever eaten. And this chicken—" he held up a chicken leg "—is so crispy."

"The potato salad is mine," her mother said. "I'm glad you like it. What did you bring, Shay?"

"I made my lemon ice box pie."

"Matt, you'll have to try a piece. Shay makes the best pies."

He looked at Shay as if she'd been keeping something valuable hidden from him. "I didn't know that. Is that what you handed the lady as we were going into the church?"

Shay nodded.

After that he started asking her mother and father about them and Lewisville, along with the Jackson area. He seemed interested in their remarks.

"Shay, you need to bring Matt to dinner one night. Let him have a good home-cooked meal," her mother suggested.

"Thanks. That sounds nice," Matt responded.

Shay wasn't sure how she felt about that. That sounded as if Matt might be getting too involved in her life. She didn't want to become overly attached to him.

Together they went to the dessert table. Matt filled his plate, making sure he took a large slice of the pie she'd prepared.

Back at their seats, he raised a fork full of the pie. "This is wonderful. Ms. Gladys will have to step up her game."

Shay couldn't deny the pleasure that filled her at Matt's praise. John had never said anything kind about her cooking or anything else for that matter. In hindsight she could see where he'd been far more interested in himself.

With their plates cleared away, Shay said, "We need to be getting to the ballpark."

They said their goodbyes to her parents and started toward the car. Shay said, "We'll change here. It's much nicer than in the ballfield restrooms."

When they arrived at the ballpark one of her team members was already busy handing out new team T-shirts. She grabbed hers and Matt's. As soon as he had his, he stripped out of the shirt he wore. Her mouth went dry as she stared at his toned chest before it disappeared behind the T-shirt.

"Shay, aren't you going to change your T-shirt?" Matt stuffed his shirt into his bag.

She blinked. "Yeah…uh… I'll run over to the restroom."

As she walked across the parking lot, she saw Matt on the field warming up with the other players. He looked supersexy in the T-shirt just tight enough for her to make out the valleys and dips of his chest. His sports shorts highlighted a nicely rounded butt while allowing her glimpses of thick muscled thighs and calves down to sports shoes. He'd pulled on a ball cap.

This had to stop. She refocused and headed for the field. As she joined the others tossing the ball, she called to Matt, "Hey, where'd you get the glove?"

"I found it out in the shed, which seems it has a little bit of everything in it." With a smile on his face, he pitched the ball to her.

She caught it. Her heart fluttered when he grinned at her.

CHAPTER FOUR

MATT HAD MISSED THIS. He threw the ball to second base from left field.

Before his mother remarried, he'd been on a baseball team. After that his stepfather had said that Matt playing ball was a waste of time and money. That had been the end of his ball career.

He'd liked being part of a team, the camaraderie. Most of his childhood, he'd been on the outside of the family. His stepfather had made Matt feel as if he wasn't as important to him as his own son and daughter. In college, medical school and afterward, Matt had made a point not to get too close to anyone. Except Dr. Warren who had been his mentor and friend, but even from him Matt had held his relationship with his family back. As good as Dr. Warren was to him their relationship still remained professional.

In an odd way Matt felt more a part of a

community today than he ever had. He never thought he had time for this type of activity before. He had always been studying or putting in overtime at the hospital to get ahead. Where had that gotten him when it had been his words against a senior doctor's? Without a job and starting over.

Maybe when he got to Chicago he'd seek out a place to play some ball. Yeah, like he'd have time for that. He had a whole new learning curve ahead of him.

Shay pulled their team into a circle to give them a pep talk. "I want you to play fair and have a good time." She looked around the group and grinned. "But I want us to beat these guys. We can't go home again in defeat this year. Everyone in on it?"

Those in the group whooped and hollered. Matt wasn't shocked she was such a competitor. He'd seen some of that character at the clinic. He liked that about her.

She stuck her hand out and the other men and women put theirs on top of hers. Matt joined them. "On three, say win. One, two, three."

Everyone raised their hands and shouted before they trotted out onto the field.

Matt took his position in left field while Shay went to center field.

"You okay over there?" Shay called.

"Yeah."

She grinned. "Good. Thanks for helping us out."

"You're welcome."

Matt hoped his very rusty skills didn't fail him. He survived the top of the first inning, and they went in to bat. That part of the game became problematic for him when Shay stepped into the batter's box. He watched her hips sway as she adjusted to get a good foot position. He swallowed. He shouldn't notice her that way. They were colleagues. The only problem was the longer he stayed around Shay the more difficult it became to ignore her appeal.

At the bottom of the fifth inning with their team down by one run, his turn to bat came up with bases loaded. The team called encouragement as he stepped up to the batter's box.

Above all the noise he heard Shay's voice yelling, "You've got this, Matt."

He wasn't so sure about that, but he wanted to make her proud. Looking around the bases, then over his shoulder at the crowd and then at his teammates and Shay in particular, he settled his nerves by swinging a few times.

Not since his solo surgery had he been this nervous.

The first throw he let go over the plate.

"Strike," the umpire called.

Great. At this rate he'd humiliate himself. If he just managed a hit the game would be tied or maybe they'd go ahead.

This time the throw went wide.

"Come on, Matt. You've got this." Shay's voice stood out among the others.

He swung at the next ball. With the pop of the bat against the ball, he ran for first base. The ball hit just behind second base and rolled toward the outfield. As the players scrambled, Matt ran for second base.

Cheers went up. He stopped and watched Shay jumping up and down just outside the dugout. Their team was up by two. Gorgeous in her excitement, she jerked her cap off. Her hair flew around her face. Her shirt flipped up, revealing a tanned and fit-looking swath of skin.

Shifting his focus back to home plate and the next batter, he waited for the man to make a hit. He did and Matt ran, glad for all those regular runs he made. When he crossed home plate, Shay waited for him. Her arms circled his neck as his arms wrapped her waist.

Wiggling against him in her joy, she said into his ear, "You're our secret weapon."

The other team members joined in the celebration.

In that moment his chest swelled. It felt good being a part of something outside of the operating room. He'd known a part had been missing in his life but had no idea what. Was it possible to have this feeling more often?

By the bottom of the seventh inning, they were still holding the lead. The best player on their team, he'd soon learned, was up to bat. The pitcher threw the ball. Their man gave the ball a solid shot and it became a line-drive at the pitcher.

Seconds later the ball hit the pitcher and he stumbled forward, landing on his face.

At a run, Shay followed Matt out of the dugout. She yelled over her shoulder, "Dad, call 911 and get my bag out of my car."

Matt slid to his knees beside the man. Before he could get words out Shay joined him. Together they rolled Gil onto his back and pulled his shirt up out of the way. A discolored spot the size of a softball showed over his heart.

"Gil, it's Shay. Gil." She shook him. The man didn't answer. His lips had turned blue.

Matt snapped, "He's in commotio cordis. The ball hit him just in the right place at the right time. We have to start CPR." Matt placed one hand over the other, beginning chest compressions.

"Someone get the AED machine," Shay shouted to the crowd. She took her position at Gil's head. Leaning his head back, she checked his mouth for any obstructions. Inhaling deeply, she pinched off Gil's nose and sealed her mouth around his and breathed into him until his chest rose.

Matt continued his efforts. Not soon enough for her the crowd parted and the portable AED machine in a lime-green box was placed on the ground beside her.

One of the EMTs who had been playing for the other team joined Shay and Matt, but on the opposite side of Gil. With quick, sure hands, he opened the box and placed the sticky pads on Gil's chest.

She and Matt moved away from Gil as the machine beeped and the electric shock went into his body. Shay picked up Gil's wrist and took his pulse. "Nothing."

The EMT reset the machine.

Her father set her bag beside her. She opened it and pulled out her stethoscope.

Gil's body jumped again at the shock.

Matt picked up his wrist this time.

With the ends of the stethoscope in her ears, she placed the bell over Gil's heart. Was that a flutter? She slid the bell to the left. Yes! She looked at Matt for confirmation. His face filled with concentration and eased as a soft smile came to his lips. He nodded.

She looked around the crowd. "We've got a beat. Does anyone know how much longer on the ambulance?"

"In ten minutes," someone called.

She looked at Matt. "We have to prevent shock. We need a blanket here and something to put under his feet."

A sports bag was passed their way. Matt took it and placed it under Gil's feet. A picnic blanket appeared, and he pulled it over Gil.

Shay continued to listen to Gil's heartbeat. Thankfully it had grown stronger. They closely monitored Gil's vitals until the ambulance EMTs took over.

She and Matt saw Gil settled in the ambulance then walked over to join the crowd still lingering near the field.

"Way to go." A number of people patted them on their backs.

Matt looked as humble as she felt.

"I think we've both had enough excitement

for the day. Are you ready to head home?"
she asked Matt.

"Sure."

They picked up their belongings and
started for the car.

Less than an hour later, Shay drove up Matt's
drive.

He turned to her. "I have to say that was
one of the nicest and most interesting days
I've spent in a long time. Thanks for inviting me."

Shay nodded. "It was a good day. I could
have done without Gil getting hurt but…"

"Will you let me know how he's doing
when you hear?"

"I will."

Matt opened the door. "Thanks again. The
day was one to remember."

He stood in the drive and watched as Shay
drove away. He'd never met someone so com-
pletely dedicated to her work and her community. Shay gave them her all. The more
he got to know her, the more he wanted to
know about her. Where he'd once thought
her ordinary, now he recognized her beauty
inside and out. Her love hung in her voice
when she talked about any of her patients.
She considered them all equally important.

What would it be like to live under Shay's umbrella of care?

Later that evening the phone rang. Matt expected it would be Shay letting him know about Gil, but instead it was his mom.

"Hey, sweetheart. I haven't heard from you in a few weeks and wanted to see how you're doing."

He hadn't wanted to tell her and his step-father that he'd had to leave LA until he'd settled into his new position. He didn't want them to worry about him—or worse, be disappointed he left his job. It was important they were proud of him. "I'm fine, Mom."

"That's good to hear. How's Jenna? We'd love to meet her sometime."

His lips tightened into a line. He'd planned to marry Jenna and hadn't even introduced her to his mother. What had he been thinking? Jenna deserved better and certainly his parents had. "We broke up."

"Oh, sweetheart, what happened?" Her disappointment and concern sounded clear in her voice. His mother wanted him to have someone who loved him, to share his life with. She felt he worked too hard and didn't give enough attention to finding the right person to settle down with. Maybe that was why he'd misread Jenna.

"I decided to move to Chicago, and she didn't want to come with me."

"You're moving to Chicago? When did you decide to do that?" His mother sounded perplexed, concerned and disappointed. "Why am I just hearing about this now?"

A tinge of guilt pricked him. Was he unfair to his mother just because he didn't want to look bad in the eyes of his stepfather? He feared it was true. For years he'd worked to make the man proud. "I would've when I got there."

"You're not there now? Where are you? Matt, why do you insist on treating me, us, as if we don't care about you? As if you don't have family who love you?"

It had started when he hadn't felt like he measured up to the standards his stepfather set. He wanted to. Just once he'd like for his stepfather to say Matt had done well. "I'm in Jackson, Mississippi. I'm staying in Henry Warren's place and working in a clinic until it's time to go to Chicago."

His mother sighed heavily. "Will you tell me what happened in LA?"

"I reported another surgeon for a decision that could have killed the patient. He had more clout than me. I saw the writing on the wall and left before I was fired. The upside is I have a good position in Chicago waiting for me." Matt didn't even want to think about what his stepfather would say when he heard the explanation. He would probably think Matt should have stayed and fought for his job.

"You'll be closer to us." Excitement filled her voice. "We'll be able to see you more often. Will you come see us soon? It's been over a year since you've been home. Your brother and sister ask about you every time they call."

Every time they spoke his mother begged him to come home. He always put her off. How could he face them after telling her that story? After he gave it some time, then maybe. "I'll see about coming before I start work in Chicago."

"I'd like that." The expectant note in his mother's voice made him feel only guiltier.

"I have to go, Mom. I'll call you soon."

"I love you, Matt."

"I love you too. Bye."

Matt looked at the phone. He hated hurting his mother, but he couldn't change the years of feeling inadequate. In truth, he'd worked so many long hours for so many years he'd really had a good excuse not to visit more often. But now... He just didn't want to face them until he had his act together once more. He would go to Chicago, settle in and feel better about what happened in LA before visiting with his family. Then there might be a chance he could handle it.

He envied what he'd seen between Shay and her parents. Shay and the people she knew. Could he find that?

Moments later his phone beeped. He had an incoming text. Shay.

Gil is stable. They are keeping him overnight to be careful. Thanks for your help saving his life.

He typed back, We made a good team. Shay returned with, We did. Good night.

Why did the tension in him ease just by receiving a text from Shay? She had a way about her that just made him feel better about himself. He wanted more of that in his life.

Midafternoon Monday, he received a call from Ralph saying his car had been fixed.

As he and Shay walked out to her car that evening, he said, "My car's ready. Do you mind dropping me off at Ralph's?"

"Sure, I'll be glad to."

He slid into the passenger seat. "I'll finally be out of your hair and you can spend less time being a taxi driver."

"I haven't minded."

"I've appreciated it." Now that he'd have his car back, he'd miss their time alone before and after work. He enjoyed their talk of anticipating the day and sharing their day after work. It had been just their time.

He hopped out of the car when they arrived at the garage. "See you in the morning." Before he could close the door, he asked, "I'd like to take you to dinner Friday night to say thank you for all your help."

Her mouth dropped open. Had he surprised her? "Uh…no thanks are necessary."

"Come on, Shay. I get tired of eating alone even when the casseroles are good."

Both her hands gripped the steering wheel and she looked out the front window. "I don't date."

"As in me or in general?" He watched her.

"I'd say both."

He leaned his head farther into the car. "Could we maybe make it a business dinner between colleagues? Not call it a date, if it bothers you that much."

Her gaze returned to him. "I haven't been out with a man since I got married."

"How long ago was that?"

"Six years," she said quietly.

His forehead wrinkled while disbelief rang in his voice. "You haven't been on a date since your husband died?"

She glared at him. "Yeah. I know that sounds pitiful, but you make it sound like I have some type of rare virus."

"I'm just shocked. I figured a woman as attractive, intelligent and loved in the community as you are would have plenty of men wanting to take you out."

"I didn't say I hadn't been asked. I just haven't been interested," she said softly.

"How about making an exception for me? If you're afraid of being seen with me then how about we go to Natchez?"

Shay thought for a minute. She let go of the wheel and smiled. "No. Jackson has plenty of good restaurants."

"Then it's a date. I mean dinner get-together."

She raised her chin as if she had made a major decision. "I think I'd like to call it a date."

He suddenly felt excited about life for the first time in weeks. "A date it is."

* * *

On Friday evening Shay opened her front door to Matt with a drumming heart. She refused to admit to herself or anyone else how much she'd looked forward to the evening. Sheree had asked more than once why she wore such a smile.

She'd glanced at Matt one too many times at lunch and had gotten caught. Sheree had winked at her and grinned. Just before Sheree had left for the day, she'd popped her head in the office and looked around.

"Okay. What gives between you and the hunky doctor?"

"Nothing."

"Those looks you keep giving him isn't nothing." Sheree pinned her with a look.

"He invited me to dinner to say thank you for driving him around is all." Shay sounded defensive even to her own ears.

"If he just wanted to say thank you he could've bought you a card. It's way past time you started living again. This is a good time to do that. And a great guy to do it with."

Shay went hot, embarrassment washing over her.

"I'll want to hear all about it on Monday. Every little detail. Have a good time. Don't do anything I wouldn't do." Sheree chuckled.

Over the next few hours Shay built the evening up into more than it should be. Now she was confident it couldn't live up to her imagination.

"Come in." She opened the door wider for Matt. "All I need to do is get my purse."

Matt stepped inside and closed the door. "Interesting."

Shay looked around the room trying to find what brought on that remark. "What?"

"This isn't at all what I expected. It doesn't look like you at all."

"How's that?" She looked over the space at the brown sofa and black leather chairs with the plaid pillows. Chrome tables sat at each end of the sofa and a large one served as a coffee table. It looked as it always had.

"I just thought you'd—" he shrugged "—have floral pillows all around. I've seen you in a number of shirts with flowers on them. Even the dress you are wearing has them."

He'd paid that much attention to her clothing? "This is what my husband liked."

Matt shook his head as if disappointed. "You haven't changed it in all this time?"

Outside the entrance to the restaurant, Shay watched as Matt walked around the front of his car to open the door for her. He looked so handsome dressed in his green plaid collared shirt, navy jacket and tan pants. Even his confident walk of a man who knew and understood himself drew her attention. She'd bet wherever he went he had no trouble finding dates.

He opened the door for her. "Ready?"

She nodded. Something about being with Matt built her self-confidence, which had been demolished by John's defection.

He placed his hand at her back and directed her toward the doors of the building. It felt nice to have personal contact. She'd missed it. For a long time, she'd kept to herself. Fearing she couldn't trust her judgment where males were concerned. Still, she should be careful not to read more into the evening than it was. A friendly meal between friends.

Matt said close to her ear, "You look lovely."

Shay had tried to suppress her excitement over the evening, but despite that she'd taken great care to look nice, wearing a dress she'd been saving for a special occasion. The simple, flowing material with little flowers everywhere flattered her. The fact he'd noticed made her feel good. She shouldn't have been surprised because she'd noticed his attention to detail when seeing patients. He'd taken special pains with Joey. "You look nice too."

He stroked his beard. "I did take the time for a little trim."

"I like it." His lips continued to draw her attention. Right now, they were lifted in a sexy grin that joined the twinkle in his eyes. The man knew he appealed to her. That kind of exposure made her uncomfortable. She had kept those emotions locked away for a long time. If she couldn't trust a man she'd known most of her life, how could she possibly trust one she'd known for only a few weeks?

She wasn't surprised Matt hadn't picked a simple café but instead had chosen a restaurant with white tablecloths and flickering candles, located beside the Pearl River. It fit his personality more than a diner. "This is a nice place. I've never been here before."

"Let's hope it's good. Ms. Gladys said it was the best place in town."

She grinned. "Ms. Gladys, huh?"

He shrugged. "It seems she reads all the restaurant reviews. Who would have thought?"

"You never know how people can surprise you."

His gaze shifted away. "I guess you don't.

I have to be honest I double-checked it on the internet, but she was right about the reviews."

"Then I'm looking forward to my meal." Shay had already been anticipating spending time with him. Too eagerly.

Matt looked out the large picture window. "This area fascinates me. I've never lived in a place that makes you want to slow down and appreciate life."

"Where have you lived?" She saw his wince as if he'd made a mistake. Did he not want to talk about himself?

"Mostly in the Midwest. A few places in Indiana. My stepfather had to move a couple of times for his job."

Crossing her arms on the table and looking across at him, she leaned forward. "I think, Dr. Chapman, there's more to you than is obvious."

"Isn't that the case with everyone?" He relaxed in his chair. "But I am flattered you're so interested in me."

He made that sound as if she wanted to know about him for personal reasons. Shay narrowed her eyes. "Let's just call it Deep South curiosity."

Matt quirked a brow. "That's all?"

"Yeah. Growing up and living in the same

area most of my life, I'm used to knowing about everyone."

The waiter came to take their drink order. Afterward Matt said, "I'd like to know a little more about you."

"A little is all you'll probably get. Almost anyone you ask in Lewisville can tell you about me."

"Have you ever lived anywhere but Lewisville?"

"I moved to Houston, Texas, to go to school."

He watched her as if absorbing every word. "Did you go to the University of Texas Medical School?"

"I did."

The waiter returned with their drinks and took their food order.

Matt took a sip of his drink. "I don't think I've said this before, but I think you're a really great doctor. What you're doing at the clinic is admirable. The staff respect you and the patients adore you. More than one has acted disappointed when they had to see me instead of you."

Warmth flowed through her. She worked hard to make the clinic successful. His praise mattered. "Thanks. I wish we could do more. It's a shame a person needing medical care has to come stand in line all day to be seen. I need at least one more doctor if not two. In fact, I have a couple of doctors interviewing next week. I want to have one in place before you leave. I'm sorry. I've obviously forgotten how to act on a date, talking about work."

"You're fine. There's nothing wrong with being passionate about your work. I certainly am."

"Yeah, but there are other things in life."

"I don't take much time for those. I haven't even been out to explore Jackson since my car was in the shop. It's the capital and I haven't seen the sights. My family used to count off the state capitals we visited." His thoughts seemed to leave their space and time for a moment. "You know I've not thought of that in a long time."

"Then you should see it. I'm ashamed I haven't offered to show you around. I was taught to do better." Why hadn't she? Because she had been too afraid to take a chance on being with a man? "Why don't I make that up to you tomorrow afternoon."

"Tomorrow?" He sounded surprised she'd offered.

"I have a garden club meeting in the morning, but I could do it tomorrow afternoon around one."

"Garden club? That sounds interesting." He grinned.

Shay's eyes narrowed, daring him to say more. "Don't be laughing at me. I'm trying to learn something new. I don't exactly have a green thumb."

He raised a hand as if to ward her off. "Tomorrow afternoon sounds great."

"I'll come get you. It's easier for me to drive because I know the way and don't have to give you directions." She picked up her napkin and placed it in her lap.

"Sounds like a plan. I look forward to it."

The waiter returned with their meals. They spent a few minutes quietly eating.

"How's your pasta?" Matt asked as he cut a slice of his steak.

"Very good. How's your food?" Shay looked over at his almost clean plate.

"Good." He grinned. "I'll have to let Ms. Gladys know."

She leaned toward him as if she were going to tell him a secret. "You do know everyone in your neighborhood knows by now that we're having dinner together."

"Really?" He looked around as if he would see someone he knew.

"Really. Ms. Gladys and Ms. Adriana are

known as the biggest gossips in the neighborhood."

Matt groaned. A low sound that came from deep in his throat. It made her shiver as her blood heated. What would it be like to hear it as he nuzzled behind her ear? Her fork rattled to her plate. She really was making more of this dinner than would be healthy for her emotions.

"Is everything okay?" Matt's concerned gaze went from her face to her plate and back again.

Shay picked up her fork holding it tighter than necessary. "Fine. Just fine."

Matt watched her closely for a few moments and returned to his meal.

She had to get her equilibrium back. "Did your neighbors say anything about you mowing your grass?"

He grinned and raised his chin like a conquering hero. "Let's just say I got a banana cream pie out of it."

"They're going to have you fattened up before you leave for Chicago. Uh, not that you don't look great as you are." She wanted to drop through the floor. Not since John had she ever been so fixated on a man. "I'm sorry that didn't come out exactly right."

"I knew what you meant." The lines at his

eyes became more prominent and those lips she liked so much quirked up at one corner. "Not that I don't like that you noticed."

Heat washed through her as she tried to focus on her meal.

"Would you like to have some dessert?" Matt asked.

"I'm so full I don't think I should."

"Why don't you share some of mine?" Matt picked up the menu the waiter had just put on the table. He didn't wait for her answer before he said, "We'll have the Mississippi Mud Cake. It sounds interesting."

The waiter left them.

Matt looked at her as if asking for confirmation of his decision. "I hope I don't regret that."

"I promise you won't."

The waiter soon brought him a large slice of chocolate cake with thick chocolate pecan icing.

"This looks wonderful. *Mud* in the name is misleading." Matt took a forkful and placed it in his mouth.

Shay watched with rapt attention as his sensuous mouth closed around it. A look of pleasure came over his features.

He looked at her. "This might be the best thing I've ever eaten. Don't you want some?"

Shay laughed. "I'm afraid to take any. You might fight me if I do."

"Here." He scooped up another forkful and offered it to her. "This is too good to miss."

She hesitated a moment then took the offering. "It is good."

"Good is an understatement." He ate more cake.

"Do you have someone special who bakes for you?"

"No. I don't have a great track record where my personal life is concerned. A number of ex-girlfriends. No wives or children. Which is just as well. Let's not ruin this delicious dessert by talking about that."

An interesting answer. There was more to Matt than he let on. Had he been as hurt as she?

Soon after they were on their way home. Shay couldn't get away from what Matt had said about having a personal life. She might have known a deep heartache, but she still dreamed of having a forever relationship. Along with that she wanted children, to have a family of her own. From Matt's glib answer he had no interest in those. For some reason that made her sad.

Matt took her away from her thoughts by

asking, "Will you tell me about your husband, Shay?"

She didn't want to do that. If he wasn't going to share why should she? Because she wanted him to understand why she'd not been on a date in so long. Maybe if she shared, he would too, eventually. More than anything she wanted to know more about him. "What do you want to know?"

"Where did you meet him?"

That question surprised her. She fully expected him to ask her how John died. "We were high school sweethearts. You know… the hometown hero quarterback and the head cheerleader love story. We won the state championship our senior year. We were the golden couple." They had been. She'd been so wrapped up in that ideal she couldn't see anything else.

"There's a lot to live up to in there."

Matt seemed to see what others never had, including her parents and especially not John's. A note in his voice implied he understood from experience. "Yeah, a whole lot. We went off to the University of Texas together. Him on a football scholarship and me on an academic one. Our parents were not only proud of us, but all of Lewisville seemed invested in us. We were the couple who couldn't fail."

Matt said nothing, but she had no doubt she had his complete attention. His profile remained intent on the road, but he looked at her every chance he got.

"Since I had more school to be a doctor, John decided he'd go into the US Marines while I was in med school. I would finish and he would get out then we'd come home and start building our life together. When we married John had one more year to serve. The entire town was at the wedding. Afterward John left on his first overseas deployment."

"No honeymoon?"

"One night in New Orleans." It had been a wonderful night. Life looked bright and wide-open back then. "He returned six months later but went back. He didn't return."

Matt reached over and took her hand, giving it a squeeze. "I'm really sorry."

Could she tell him the entire sordid story? She removed her hand. "The town is talking about putting up a statue in his honor."

"Oh, wow. That's an even harder cloud to live under. Forever being the wife of a hero. How do you feel about that?"

"He earned it. John saved men's lives fighting for his country." He didn't earn hero status in other parts of his life, though.

Matt pulled into her drive and turned the car off. After studying her a moment, he said, "I hear a *but* in there."

Shay sighed. She shouldn't make such a big deal out of telling him. Everyone knew. Someone would eventually tell him. She took a deep breath. "He'd been having an affair. He told me to expect divorce papers on the day he left."

Matt didn't say anything for a few moments.

Even with the years that had passed she still couldn't believe how John had humiliated her by having an affair. Her heart still hurt. Well, she'd managed to put a cloud of gloom over the end of the evening. She opened the door. "I just dropped an egg on a good time. Sorry. Thanks for the evening out."

Shay made it halfway up the walk before Matt caught her. He cupped her elbow, stopping her. "You know it was his loss. You were, are, too good for him."

She gave Matt a sad smile. "Thanks for that. You'd think after all this time I wouldn't let it upset me."

His hand slipped down her arm to hold her

hand. "Rejection is rejection. No one likes to be on the receiving end. We carry the pain around with us."

Matt sounded like he understood better than most. Shay's eyes found his. "You're a nice guy, Matt Chapman."

"You're not bad yourself." He studied her for a moment. His focus dropped to her lips.

Was he going to kiss her? Did she want him to?

He stepped back. "I had a really nice time tonight. I'm looking forward to tomorrow afternoon."

CHAPTER FIVE

MATT STOOD IN the yard talking to Ms. Gladys when Shay turned into his driveway. He had walked over to help the older woman pull her garbage can back to the house. The woman's interest in his comings and goings he found a little disconcerting, but she was nice enough. He put it down to loneliness.

"I have to go, Ms. Gladys. Shay's going to show me Jackson's sights. Hey, I appreciate your suggestion of a restaurant. It was every bit as good as you said it would be."

He glanced over to see Shay coming toward them, a flowing dress dancing around her legs. She wore all that silky hair down. Clips held it back near her ears. She looked as fresh and lovely as a clear brook did to a thirsty man.

He'd wanted to kiss her last night. She'd looked so sad. Wanted to reassure her she was desirable. But that wasn't the only reason. He was attached to her, liked her. Yet he shouldn't start anything with Shay. He'd just ended a relationship where he thought he would marry. Shay would want more than he could offer. The timing, the place, the needs were all wrong. It was best he kept his distance.

Shay wrapped Ms. Gladys in a hug. "It's so good to see you. It's been so long."

"It has been a while, honey. How's your uncle doing?" She continued to hold one of Shay's hands.

"Uncle Henry's doing great. I'll be sure to tell him you asked about him."

The older woman's cheeks pinkened.

Matt grinned. Did Ms. Gladys have a thing for Henry Warren? Matt finished pulling the can to the house and returned to the women.

Shay looked at him. "We better get going if we're going to see everything I have planned. I hope you've got your walking shoes on."

He pursed his lips in thought as if acting unsure about going with her. "So, this is going to be sightseeing and an exercise class. This may be more than I bargained for."

Shay grinned. "Yeah, we're going to do a walking tour."

"You two have a good time." Ms. Gladys waved and headed inside her house.

Shay drove them the short distance downtown.

"I'm not known for sightseeing," Matt said as he looked around as they moved through a business district. "My family did do some while I was growing up. I got out of the habit when I started college. Medical school didn't leave me any time. When I had some hours off all I wanted to do was sleep."

"Well, today, I'm going to wake up your sleeping tourist."

"So where are we headed?"

"We're gonna start down by the capitol. We don't have time today to go into the museums, but we'll just have to settle for a good overview."

Shay continued down what he did know was the main street. She took an open parking place. "Okay, this is where the walking part of the tour starts."

They joined the other people on the wide sidewalk. They strolled past small businesses and large department stores toward the huge four-storied official-looking white building, which was obviously a government building, surrounded by a green lawn.

Shay raised her hand like a TV game hostess. "This is the capitol building of Mississippi. It was built in 1903. If we were here on a weekday, we could go inside, but today we just have to appreciate it from out here. Let's go this way."

"You really do like history, don't you?"

She stopped and looked at him. "Am I boring you? Please tell me if I am."

"No, I'm enjoying this." More than that he enjoyed spending time with her.

"If you'll look right over there—" she pointed across the street "—you'll see that we have our own clock tower and gargoyles just like Notre Dame. My favorite is the one on that corner."

"Have you ever been to Paris and seen the real Notre Dame?" Matt looked at the angry-looking animal squatting on the corner of the building.

"No. But I'd love to go sometime. Right now, all my focus is on the clinic. Maybe one day." Her sigh lingered in the air.

"I've never been either. I always thought I'd like to see the city."

"Now, over in this direction is my favorite building in town. The old capitol building. It was built in 1846."

The box-shaped building with a green

dome did have a simple authority to it that appealed. "It's nice."

"We can go in here. You need to see the rotunda. It's gorgeous."

Shay's eyes lit up. He couldn't imagine the rotunda being more beautiful than her at that moment. She had started to put a spell on him.

They walked up the wide steps and through massive doors. Inside, round columns created a rotunda with the dome allowing light in from above.

Matt watched as Shay walked around the area enthralled.

"Can you imagine what it was like to come here in your finest dress and be waltzed around this beautiful room?"

Matt chuckled. "I had no idea you were such a romantic."

Shay looked at him. "I haven't thought about it, but I guess I am. Kind of sappy, isn't it?"

"Charming is what I was thinking."

She looked at him as if she saw something she hadn't before. "Thanks for not making fun of me."

Did people question the softer side of her often? "And thanks for sharing something special with me. I'm honored."

She smiled. "Come, we have a little way to walk to our next stop."

When they had to cross a busy road, Matt took her hand. She glanced at him, but didn't pull away. Back on a sidewalk he kept her hand firmly clasped in his. Soon her hand relaxed in his.

They walked in silence for a while. As they came up to a grand house Shay announced, "This is the governor's mansion. It was built in 1842 in the Greek Revival style. And you have the sum total of my knowledge. I went in it when I was in the fifth grade on a field trip, but I don't remember much about it other than it was big."

"You never wanted to dance here?"

She thought for a minute. "Nope. It's always been at the old capitol building. Now I think it's time for the tour guide to give the tourist a rest and treat him to an ice cream."

"That sounds good."

"On the way to LeFleur's Bluff park we'll pass Eudora Welty's house—she was one of Mississippi's great literary authors."

He knew that name. "I had to read one of her stories when I was an undergrad. I liked it better than most."

Shay's chin came up proudly. "I've read everything she wrote."

Matt shook his head. "Why am I not surprised."

She tugged on his hand. "Let's go get that ice cream." At the cart outside the park, she bought them each a cone. Handing one to Matt she said, "Only a small one this time. We have to save room for dinner. There's a bench over there that's empty. Let's go get it."

Matt licked the cream before it ran down the cone as they sat down. "You sounded just like a mother a minute ago."

"I hope to be one someday."

"I'm surprised you aren't already." He had stepped into an area that wasn't any of his business.

"I wanted to be. John said we needed to wait until he was out of the service." Her voice turned bitter. "But apparently with the right woman that didn't matter. It turns out the woman he was having an affair with was pregnant."

Matt put his arm around her shoulder and gave her a gentle hug. There were no words to fix the hurt in her voice. When he eased his hold she slid away from him.

They watched families and couples go by on the walking path along with a few individuals out for a hot afternoon run.

Finally, she said, her tone having returned

to normal, "Can you name a superfamous singer who's from Mississippi?"

He thought for a moment. "No."

She laughed. "Elvis."

"I thought he was from Memphis, Tennessee."

She sat straighter. "I'll have you know he was born in Tupelo, Mississippi."

"My stepfather used to dance my mother around the kitchen to Elvis's love songs." He would give credit to his stepfather for one thing—he did obviously love Matt's mom. "Do you like Elvis?"

"Yeah. Of course, I do. I've even seen his movies."

The sky rumbled. It had darkened while they had been sitting there.

"I think we should be heading back. If we don't, we might get wet." Shay stood.

On their way out of the park they threw their garbage in a can. He took her hand again. At the next roll of thunder big drops of rain started to fall.

"We better find some cover," Shay squealed.

At the next storefront with an indented entrance Matt pulled her into the space. The building was dark. It was just the two of them when the sky opened up and the rain fell full force.

As the wind picked up, he tugged her closer to the door, gaining more protection.

"This shouldn't last long." Shay shivered.

When she shook again, he took her into his arms putting himself between the worst of the weather and her. She accepted his help and snuggled into him. It felt right to protect her, to have her in his arms.

Shay's shoulders shook.

"Are you laughing?"

Her gaze met his, her eyes shining with humor. "This reminds me of those 1940s movies where the couple runs in out of the rain and the guy…"

"Kisses the girl?"

For a moment, they simply stared at each other. Shay's fingers curled into his shirt as he lowered his head, as his lips found her warm damp ones. A soft sigh floated from her. Her arms tightened, bringing her snugly against him. His tongue traveled the seam of her mouth and to his great satisfaction she opened for him. He took her invitation and found heaven.

The honking of a car horn made them jerk apart.

He looked into Shay's eyes. Uncertainty filled them. It wasn't what he wanted to see.

She looked beyond him. "Uh… I think

the worst is over now. We can start walking again."

Shay started down the street, giving him no choice but to follow. He wanted things to go back to the way they had been between them. The easy friendship. Had he ruined that by kissing her? Shay had been enjoying it. He certainly had.

"Thanks for showing me around this afternoon. I have to say, it's been nice to gather my thoughts and rest."

"That's good to hear, but once you get to Chicago are you planning to pick up where you left off?"

He shrugged a shoulder. "I'll have to pick up my pace compared to here if I plan to get back to the same position I held in LA and eventually to the head of the program."

Shay looked at him. "Why's that so important?"

That was a good question.

Shay wasn't sure why she had been peppering Matt with questions. Maybe it was to cover up the effect his kiss had on her. Her knees still felt like jelly. She shouldn't have kissed him. Where could something between them go?

What she needed to do was get over it and

move on. It wouldn't happen again. Why did the thought of that being true make her sad?

When Matt would have kept walking, she grabbed his arm, but quickly let it go. "Hold up. This is where we're going to get supper."

She pulled the diner door open. "This place is famous for its tacos and tapas. I love to have a chance to eat here." She smiled at him. "And you've given me that opportunity."

Shay spoke to the hostess about needing a table.

"Why don't we eat outside under the awning?" Matt suggested. "That way you won't get cold in here in the air-conditioning."

"That's a good idea." Had John ever been that considerate of her? Not that she could remember. They followed the waitress out to the patio. The rain had only made the air more sauna-like than cool.

They were shown to a wood-and-chrome table off to themselves. The restaurant had started filling up for the evening. They ordered their drinks.

"Thanks for thinking about this," Shay said. "It's much nicer out here."

They both looked at the menus the waitress had left. She soon returned with their drinks and they placed their order.

Shay crossed her arms and leaned on the

table. "Why did you leave LA? From all I can tell you were successful there. I did look you up."

Matt leaned back in the curl-backed chrome chair that matched the table and watched her for a moment. Was he deciding if he should tell her? Trust her? "I had a disagreement with a senior surgeon."

"Disagreement, huh?"

"It was a little more than that. We were in the middle of a procedure and he was making an incision that would endanger the patient and I said so."

She winced. "I bet that didn't go well."

"It didn't. I had to report him to the medical board."

She hissed in a breath.

"Yeah. Before the hearing he used his clout with those he could, and his word stood over mine. The board sided with him. I was the new kid questioning the senior surgeon. I knew my time there was limited even if I was right. I'd been approached about a position in Chicago last year so I called to see if they might still be interested in me."

"That must've been tough." Wow. This wasn't the average man.

"Yeah, but the patient always has to come

first." He picked up his drink and took a swallow.

"I agree, but I still admire you for standing up for what was right when it couldn't have been easy. To disrupt your entire life and career to stand by your convictions is asking a lot. I know many who wouldn't. It takes a special man."

He fingered the moisture on the side of the glass. "I don't know that I did anything special. I felt I didn't have a choice. It's what I was taught to do."

A man with principles, and humble too. If his kiss hadn't gotten her, what she'd just learned about him would've. The more she knew about Matt the better she liked him. Not a good thing. Her heart could get in trouble. "Your parents did a good job with teaching integrity."

He said nothing for a moment as if he was deep in thought. "I guess they did. My mother is a good woman who has integrity, but it was my stepfather who insisted I admit when I had done something wrong. When there was a kid in the neighborhood being bullied he said it was important to take up for those who couldn't take up for themselves. I've not thought about that for a long time.

"The problem was that I had basically

called my boss out. In the three seconds it took to say something my career went into a tailspin." Sadness filled his voice.

"I'm sorry that happened to you. Still, I'm impressed you did the right thing. Others might not have in that situation."

His gaze met hers. "I bet you would have. My mom has been begging me for years to move closer. She'll be pleased to have me in Chicago."

"You never say anything about your father."

"He died when I was three. Mom remarried when I was eight." His words were fla

By his facial expression and tone of voi she'd save any discussion about that later. "At least your moving closer to h is something good coming out of bad."

Matt sat straighter and looked dire her. "Has something good come out for you?"

How like him to turn her word "Yeah. Because of what John did ar sip and sad looks, I throw myself ing the clinic."

"You've done a great job w what have you done for yours

"I don't know. I'd like to

gargoyles on Notre Dame, the Swiss Alps. One day have a family."

Matt leaned back again and watched her for a moment. The waitress bringing their food changed the atmosphere between them. As they ate, their conversation turned to movies they had seen, and TV shows they watched.

Later, Shay pulled into his driveway. It had just turned dark enough for the streetlight to come on.

"Would you like to come in? Watch some TV for a while?" Matt watched her.

Shay hesitated a moment before saying, "No, I better be getting home. It's getting late anyway."

"I really enjoyed my afternoon and dinner. Thanks for showing me around. If you ever want to give up medicine, you'd make a great tour guide." He grinned.

Matt really did have the best smile. "I enjoyed it too. It has been too long since I visited those places."

"Shay, about that kiss—"

"Don't worry about it. We both know it wasn't a good idea."

The back of his hand brushed her cheek. "Why?"

"I don't... I don't think we need to start

something that neither one of us can finish. You're only gonna be here for a few more weeks and the last thing I need is another heartbreak."

His eyes held an earnest look. "I don't plan to break your heart."

"I'm sure you don't, but that doesn't mean it won't happen." Shay knew herself. She could so easily fall for him.

Matt leaned closer. His warm, musky scent filled her nose. "You like me that much?"

Shay closed her eyes and swallowed, hard. All she had to do was lean forward just a little and her lips would touch his. "Yeah."

"Will you look at me, Shay?"

Shay shook her head. If she did, she'd disappear into his eyes.

"Please."

At his pleading tone, she opened her eyelids. "I like you too, Shay. I can't offer you more than here and now but that doesn't mean I don't care about you."

A lovely warmth washed through her.

"Think about it." He kissed her forehead. "See you Monday at work. Good night."

Shay drove away with hands shaking and a flutter like a hummingbird flying in her

middle. How would she survive being around
Matt for the next few weeks? Did she really
want to resist him?

CHAPTER SIX

MATT HADN'T RESTRAINED himself this much since he'd been a teenager and wanted to yell at his stepfather. He'd wanted to take Shay into the house and show her what it could be like between them. Just from their short kiss he had no doubt it would be powerful.

Sunday he'd resisted calling or texting her to give her room to think. It had made for a long day. On Monday she'd acted as if nothing had happened between them and he followed her lead, yet he caught her watching him more than once. She wasn't as immune to him as she seemed. He could be patient—for a while.

Tuesday at lunch Shay said to the table in general, "I have a couple of doctors coming in for interviews this afternoon."

"Anyone we know?" Sheree asked.

"I don't think so." Shay picked up her

sandwich. "A Dr. Stevie Brown and a Dr. Kurt Willis."

"I know Dr. Willis. He's a nice guy. Really good," one of the nurses said. "Really cute too."

Shay grinned and said flippantly, "Which is always important for patient care."

"It's nice to know what's considered important to you ladies. Not all the years of training," Matt groused before he finished his leftover casserole.

"Hey, what're you complaining about," Sheree said. "You certainly qualify in the looks department." She stood. As she did, she placed a hand on his shoulder. "We just need to find one as fine as you."

"Thanks. But I'm not sure I feel any better."

Shay grinned at him as if she were enjoying his discomfort. "Seriously, your skills will be hard to replace."

Why should it matter to him that Shay was trying to find a replacement for him? That had been the agreement all along. He shoved his lunch bowls into his bag. What he didn't want was some guy coming in and gaining Shay's interest as well. Why not? He had no hold on her. She would move on when he was gone. The idea left a bad taste in his mouth.

Between patients he saw Shay showing

around a woman. So, Stevie was female. Later he saw her with a tall blond man that even Matt had to admit had better than average looks.

Sheree walked up beside him wearing a teasing smile. "He looks like he might fit in here perfectly."

Matt snarled and walked off with the sound of Sheree's laughter following him. Jealousy wasn't something he was familiar with. He'd never felt one ounce of it with Jenna. He wasn't in any real relationship with Shay and jealousy was running wild in his blood. Would this blond doctor be the man that opened the world up again for Shay?

Matt hated the idea but what could he say or do? Soon he would be leaving. They would be living hundreds of miles away from each other. He'd be spending countless hours trying to build his career. Matt glanced at Shay and the doctor. Maybe it was just as well. Anyone would be a better choice for Shay than Matt. Most of all he wanted her happiness.

He knocked on the exam room door with more force than necessary. There were patients to see.

Wednesday afternoon he and Shay were

on their way to see patients after lunch when Sheree met them in the hallway.

"Matt, Mr. Clayton is here requesting to see you."

He looked at Shay. People didn't request to see him. They usually asked for Shay. "Who? Oh, yeah, the man who hurt his hand the first week I was here."

"Yes, that's the one." Sheree pointed to exam room two. "He's in there."

"I'll see him right now."

"I'd like to see him too, if it's all right with him," Shay said from behind Matt.

"I'll ask and see. Make sure it isn't something he'd rather see a male doctor about." Matt knocked on the door and entered.

Mr. and Mrs. Clayton stood with wide smiles on their faces. "We wanted to come by and say thank you."

"Thank you?" What were they talking about?

"For saving my hand." Mr. Clayton raised his bandaged hand.

"You're welcome." Matt couldn't help but be impressed they had stopped in just to see him. "Dr. Lunsford would like to see you too if that's okay?"

"Sure," the man said in his deep, gravelly voice.

Matt went to the door. "Come in. They're just here for a friendly visit."

Shay entered. "It's good to see you, Mr. Clayton. How's the hand doing?"

"Dr. Roper says it's doing great thanks to Dr. Chapman. They tell me I might have lost it altogether if it hadn't been for Dr. Chapman."

Embarrassment filled Matt at all the praise. "Do you mind if we have a look at your hand, Mr. Clayton?"

"Not at all."

Matt sat on the rolling stool while Mr. Clayton took a seat on the exam table and Mrs. Clayton took the chair. Shay stood beside him. She handed him a pair of scissors.

As Matt removed the bandage he said, "Your surgeon has kept us posted on how you have been doing. He's pleased with the results." Matt finished taking the gauze off and dropped them in the garbage can.

Gently, he took Mr. Clayton's hand in the palm of his and studied it. Shay stepped close behind him and looked over his shoulder. The mangled skin would be scarred but otherwise the hand looked as if it would recover well. "Can you move your fingers for me?"

Mr. Clayton moved the tips of his fingers. "I've been told it'll need some physical therapy but that I should get the majority of the use back."

"That's wonderful to hear."

Shea put her hand on his shoulder and gave it a squeeze.

"It does look good. I'll get the supplies and get this wrapped up again for you." Matt pushed back from the exam table.

"I'll do that," Shay said. She went to the cabinet and started pulling out what was needed.

Mrs. Clayton picked up a large basket filled with fresh vegetables that had been sitting on the floor and handed it to him. "These are for you as a thank-you. They're from our garden. Jim is known for his tomatoes."

Matt had received casseroles and pies but for some reason this simple gift meant more. This was the first time he'd ever had a patient bring him a gift for doing his job. With a lump in his throat Matt said, "Thank you. These look wonderful."

A few minutes later Matt, with Shay beside him, watched the Claytons walk toward the front door. Shay squeezed his upper arm. "Nice going, Dr. Chapman."

He looked at her. "That's the best patient visit I've ever had."

"You deserved it."

* * *

Shay had just gotten home from having dinner with her parents and changed clothes. She'd thought about going by Matt's, but stopped herself. It would have been sending the wrong message if she had. She'd drawn the boundaries and she should live with them. As Matt had been. As much as she would've liked for him to kiss her, he'd been a gentleman.

She smiled at the memory of the look on his face after the Claytons' visit. He'd been overwhelmed. Shay feared he'd not had enough admiration in his life. Matt was the type of doctor, and man, that deserved it. It was good he'd received it while working here.

Her phone rang. She picked it up.

She recognized Matt's voice even though it was little more than a groan. "I need help."

"I'm on the way." Shay scooped up her purse and ran for the car.

Twenty minutes later, of what was usually a thirty-minute trip, she pulled to a jerking stop in Matt's drive and ran for the back door. She raised a hand in Ms. Gladys's direction where she stood near the street talking to a neighbor. Not bothering to knock, Shay entered the house. "Matt, where are you?"

"In here." His voice came as little more

than a painful moan from somewhere deep in the house.

She found him sprawled on a bed with a sheet over his hips and the rest of him bare. Shay swallowed hard. Then she saw his ankles and legs and the rest of him was forgotten. They were a deep red with small marks dotting them. One calf had swollen to a painful size. Matt's arm lay across his face covering his eyes.

Her heart went out to him. "Matt, what have you done to yourself?"

He didn't remove his arm as he spoke to her. "I just mowed the grass. Some kind of ant did the rest. My legs are on fire."

"Yeah, that's because you stepped in a fire ant bed. They don't like that at all."

He raised his arm just enough to glare at her. The pain showed clearly in his eyes. "I learned that the hard way. All I did was push the mower over a mound of red dirt. The engine bogged down and quit. I was trying to restart it when something stung me. I looked down to see my shoes and ankles covered in red ants. They swarmed me. No matter how much I stomped they hung on."

"They'll do that." He sounded so pitiful Shay couldn't help but feel sorry for him.

"I ran for the house pulling my clothes off as I went."

"I bet Ms. Gladys liked that," Shay murmured.

"It didn't matter. I had to get those things off me. I wore my shorts into the shower. The water was the only way to get them off. Hot water only made things worse, so I ended up with a cold shower. That didn't help much. Then I called you."

Shay put her bag on the bed beside him. "I'll see if I can make you more comfortable. It looks like you're allergic to them. Are you having any trouble breathing?"

"No."

"If you do start having trouble, we'll need to get you to the emergency room. I'll give you an antihistamine and some pain medicine and see if that helps."

His arm went back over his eyes again. "I doubt that's possible. This is embarrassing but I'm so miserable I'll take any help I can get."

"I'm sorry. You really must be in pain." She squeezed his hand. "I'll have you feeling better in a few minutes." Shay dug through her bag and found the medicine. "I need to get you some water to take these with. Don't move."

"Like I could," Matt grumbled.

She went to the kitchen and soon returned with the water. She handed Matt the pills and he quickly swallowed them.

"I don't have any steroid cream with me. I'm going to ice your legs. If your leg swells any more then I'll have to go to the clinic and get the cream. For now, I'll wait and see. Do you have any freezer bags?"

"What?" he muttered.

"Then I guess not. I'll see what I can find in the kitchen." She'd be surprised if there was much in the house based on what she'd seen so far. "I'll be right back."

The house wasn't much different than the last time she'd been in it. All the same furniture, mostly secondhand stuff. There were two other bedrooms along the hall but there wasn't any furniture in them. Uncle Henry must figure his renters would want their own bedroom furniture.

In the kitchen she checked the freezer of the refrigerator and found no bags of frozen vegetables. At least the ice tray was full. Pulling out drawers and looking in the cabinets, she found a couple of plastic bags from the grocery store. She filled them with some ice, tied them closed and returned to Matt.

From the bath, she grabbed a towel and

draped it over his legs then placed the bags on his legs, arranging the ice so that it covered as much of his skin as possible.

Matt made a moan of pleasure. "Thanks."

"Better?"

"Yeah. At least you put the fire out for a while," he murmured.

She pulled the sheet farther up his chest and brushed his hair from his forehead. He had a fever. "Get some sleep. It'll help."

His hand caught hers and held it for a moment. "Thanks, Shay."

"Not a problem. I'm just sorry you feel so bad." When his breathing turned even, she pulled a stuffed chair from the corner and positioned it beside the bed. She would stay with him as long as he needed her.

There was a knock at the door. Shay hurried toward it, not wanting the person to wake Matt. Halfway there she realized what she wore. At Matt's call she hadn't thought to change clothes in her urgency to get to his house. Now she realized she wore a knit tank-top with no bra and very short cutoff jeans she'd pulled on to get comfortable.

Running back to Matt's room, she shook out one of his dress shirts lying on the chest of drawers and pulled it on, tying it at her waist and rolling up the sleeves.

Another insistent knock had her dashing to the door. Ms. Gladys stood on the other side.

"Is everything okay? I saw you running in a while ago. I got worried."

"Matt stepped into a fire ant bed and didn't know what they were. Turns out he's allergic to them."

The old woman sighed. "I should've known. The lawnmower was left out in the yard. He's been so good about mowing the grass lately."

"He's eaten up pretty badly and running a fever." Shay hoped to placate the woman, so she'd soon leave.

"Is there anything I can do?" Ms. Gladys moved forward as if she planned to enter the house, but Shay blocked the doorway.

"Right now, I think we're fine. Matt's sleeping."

"You let me know if you need me. Matt's a nice guy. I've become fond of him."

So had Shay. Too much so. "Thanks, Ms. Gladys. I need to get back to Matt right now. He doesn't need to be alone until his fever is gone."

"All righty, I'll go." The old woman slowly walked away.

"Hey, Ms. Gladys."

The woman turned to look at Shay. "Yes?"

"I bet Matt would enjoy some of your soup when he's feeling better."

A bright smile came to the woman's mouth. "I'll fix him some."

Shay had lived with this type of helpful yet sometimes nosy neighbor situation her entire life. There was a time when it bothered her, but it had nice aspects as well. Being cared for by others mattered.

Returning to Matt, she found him resting easy. His legs were still bright red and swollen. The fire ants had really done a job on him.

Shay touched his forehead. The fever remained. That concerned her. She'd hoped it would be gone since he'd had medicine to bring it down. Matt slept soundly enough as she hadn't woken him with her touch. She didn't feel good about leaving him yet. She'd stay a little while longer. Thankfully she kept a book in her purse for times like these. With it in hand she settled on the well-worn sofa to read.

An hour went by before she heard Matt stir. He went into the bathroom. At the sound of him coming out she moved down the hall calling out, fearing he wasn't back in bed yet. "Hey, how're you feeling?"

"Awful. My legs are on fire."

She entered his room. He'd returned to the bed and was in the process of adjusting the towel and ice on his legs. The sheet collected low on his hips just covering his groin. Shay made herself look away. She was a doctor. She'd seen naked men before. But this wasn't just any patient.

"Lie back and I'll do that." The words came out harsher than she intended.

To her amazement, he did as she asked without argument, indicating how uncomfortable he must be. Thankfully, he pulled the sheet up to under his arms as she went about seeing to his legs. "I need to get some more ice. Are you hungry?"

"Yeah, I guess so. What I really am is thirsty."

"Then I'll be right back with ice and something to drink." She headed out the door.

"Hey, Shay."

She looked back at him. "I like those sexy shorts and you look cute in my shirt."

Matt grinned for the first time in hours. A flush of color came to Shay's cheeks at his observation. He liked it when he got the best of her. She appeared so self-assured all the time but when he made any suggestion of attraction between them, she acted all shy as if she didn't want to think about the spark between them.

He settled back, waiting for her to return. He hated that she had to take care of him, but even he realized he'd messed up when he'd gotten into that ant hill. As bad as he felt, it didn't mean he was unaware of Shay's charms, especially those unbounded breasts she covered with his shirt.

Soon Shay returned with ice in bags and a large drink in her hand. She handed him the glass and fussed around his legs. He checked his phone while she left briefly; then she returned with a slice of chicken potpie for him. Thank goodness for neighbors. Sitting up, he leaned back against the headboard, making sure his waist remained covered. She handed him the plate then took a seat in the chair.

He picked up the fork. "Thanks for taking care of me."

"You've already said that." She watched him as if ready to jump in to help him.

"I mean it. Tell me about these fire ants. Who knew ants could be so vicious?"

She leaned back as if settling into a subject she was comfortable with. "Hundreds of years ago they rode into America on a banana boat from South America. They got off in New Orleans or someplace on the coast and started their march north."

Matt grinned. "You make them sound like a human army."

"They're more destructive." She pointed at his legs. "You should know. I've seen small children hospitalized from being bitten by fire ants. They're awful. Haven't you seen the mounds of dirt one or two feet high in the fields?"

He swallowed. "Yeah, but I didn't know what they were."

Shay gave him a wry smile. "I bet you do now."

"That I do. Who was at the door earlier?" He finished off his potpie.

She grinned and took his plate. "Ms. Gladys. She was concerned about her favorite neighbor."

He raised his brows. "Was she?"

"She would've come in to see you if I'd let her." Shay placed the plate on the dresser.

"She might have seen more than she wanted to." Matt adjusted the sheet.

Shay grinned. "Knowing her, she wouldn't have minded."

"Still, I'm glad you didn't let her in." He paused for a drink.

She moved to stand.

He grabbed her hand. "Stay and talk to me for a while."

She settled on the edge of the chair. He didn't like her being skittish around him. He thought they'd gotten past that. "Tell me about your family. I met your mother and father, but do you have any brothers or sisters?"

"I have a brother who lives in Memphis. He and his wife have two children—who are the best, by the way. They come down when they can but it's not often enough for me, Mom and Dad. How about you? Brothers and sisters?"

He could tell by the look on her face and the sound of her voice she loved them dearly. He was sure he didn't have those tones when he spoke of his family. "Both. I have a half brother who lives in California and a half sister who lives in St. Louis. I haven't seen either of them in years."

Her eyes widened and she leaned forward as if she didn't believe him. "Oh, wow. That's awful."

How like Shay to say exactly what she thought. "I've been busy."

"I'm never too busy for people I love." Her mouth turned down in horror. "I shouldn't have said that."

Shay wouldn't be, but then she knew what

it was to meet their expectations, to make them proud. He didn't. Despite him being a doctor, he never felt he'd been enough in his stepfather's eyes. The issue in LA and changing hospitals wouldn't improve on the situation either.

Shay stood. "Let me check and see if you're still running a fever." She pulled her electric thermometer out of her bag, placing it on his forehead. When it beeped, she looked at the instrument. "It's low-grade but still there. I'll take this—" she picked up the plate "—and get you more to drink, then give you another dose of medicine. You should sleep. By morning you'll hopefully be better. I'll be here if you aren't to take you to the hospital."

"You're going to stay?" Surprise filled his voice.

"Yes. I don't want you to get worse and no one know it. I can't have you going into anaphylactic shock with no one around." She gave him a stern look.

She did care. He watched her tight behind in those short shorts as she left the room and wished he felt better.

The next thing he knew he woke to a dark room. A light came from down the hall, but the house remained quiet. He was cold and his legs itched like the devil. Climbing out of bed, he made his way to the bathroom. When he came out Shay stood in the doorway. He should have put some shorts on but didn't have the energy to look for them. In the dim light she couldn't see much.

"Hey, how're you doing?"

He got back into bed. "I'm freezing and my legs itch. Other than that, I couldn't be better."

She walked to the side of the bed and touched his forehead. "You were sleeping, and I decided to wait to give you medicine. I should've woken you."

He pulled the sheet up to his neck. Shay draped the blanket over him. "Do you have any other bedcovers?"

"No." His teeth chattered as he closed his eyes.

Shay woke against a warm body. Matt lay at her back with his arm across her waist. A ripple of shock went through her. What was she doing here? All she planned to do was help keep him warm until he settled. Heavens, she had fallen asleep. In bed. With Matt. It did feel good to have a man holding her close. It had been so long. Yet she couldn't stay here.

Heat no longer radiated off him. At least

his fever had broken. She'd removed the bags of ice, gave him pain medicine trying to make him as comfortable as possible, but he still pulled into a ball and shivered. She'd found an extra blanket in the closet, but it had done little good. He continued being miserable. Unable to sit by and watch him in misery, she'd crawled under the covers and wrapped her arms around him, intending to stay for only a few minutes.

Now here she was in bed with Matt hours later. He shifted, and she took her chance to move away, but his arm tightened. His breath was but a soft whish across her cheek. She had to get out of bed before Matt really woke. What would he think about her sleeping with him?

Matt's breathing changed. He nuzzled her neck. "Mmm…"

"Matt?" she whispered.

"Uh?"

She'd been tempted to move her head, giving him better access to her neck. His lips against her skin had her thinking and feeling things better left alone. "I need to get up."

"I like you right here," he grumbled, but his arm moved off her waist.

She slid out of bed, then looked down at him. "I, uh…didn't mean to go to sleep."

He watched her too closely. "I didn't mind."

"How're your legs feelings?" She needed to get this conversation going in another direction.

He grinned. "Better than other parts of my body."

She shivered. "Really."

He rolled to his back, the covers showing more of his chest than she would have liked. Then again, she would have liked to see more. She needed to get out of here before she got herself in trouble.

"Better I think," Matt answered.

"I'm glad to hear it. I need to go, but before I do, I should check your legs."

Matt lay back on the pillows. She pushed the covers up to reveal his calves, and he watched her as she went about examining his legs. She felt his attention as if it were a hand resting on her. The muscles in her middle quivered. Why didn't that bother her? Instead, she wanted to get back in bed with him.

Why wouldn't she let go and take what she wanted? What she believed Matt would be willing give. Because she wanted forever, and Matt wouldn't be that.

CHAPTER SEVEN

SHAY MADE IT through an unbelievable day—
barely. It had been difficult on two levels and
all because of Matt. Without his help she'd
been busier than usual and when she wasn't
seeing a patient she walked around in a haze
of what-ifs.

She wanted to say that fog had to do with
the long stint she'd gone without sex, but she
feared it had more to do with Matt in particular. Being wrapped in his arms that morning
had been enough to whet her appetite.

Having a fling wasn't like her, but she
wanted to, badly. Her life stayed under a microscope. She had an obligation to the town
who had expectations of her. Still there was
nothing like the feeling of being desired. Matt
had given her that as no one else had. Her and
John's relationship had been about youth and
dreams and being comfortable. With Matt it
was about being mature, of knowing what

she wanted; and the fact Matt made her uncomfortable in a good way. *It has been too
long since you've been held in a man's arms,
much less been kissed into oblivion.* It was
a heady experience. She could so easily get
drunk on need.

That morning when she'd come out of the
bathroom, he'd still been in bed. The temp-
tation to join him had almost taken her control. Instead, she'd gone into doctor mode
and cared for his legs. "I'm going to ask Ms.
Gladys to check on you."

"You're going to do what?" He sat up in
bed. "Are you trying to punish me?"

She narrowed her eyes and pursed her lips
as if talking to a child. "Someone needs to
check on you. To make sure you aren't running a fever."

"I'll go to work. I can make it." He grabbed
the sheet as if planning to flip it back.

"No, you won't. You need to stay off your
legs for the day. Without you at the clinic I
can't get away to see you." Her look bore into
him. "That leaves Ms. Gladys. And if I know
her, and I do, she'll see that you are fed. I already have her bringing you soup."

Matt groaned and leaned back.

"I'd suggest you get a shower now." She
glanced down at his hips barely covered by

the sheet. "And put on some clothes because ten minutes after I talk to her, she'll be over here."

He glared at her much like he had the night before. "You're enjoying this, aren't you?"

Shay grinned. "A little."

He gave her his best wolfish look that made her eyes widen. "You do know I'll have to get you back for this."

"I'm not the one who stepped in the fire ants." She stepped back toward the door.

"You can be a cold woman, Dr. Lunsford. How're you going to handle the clinic by yourself? Why don't I come in after lunch?"

"I'll deal. You need to stay off those legs *all* day. Keep in mind I'll be asking Ms. Gladys for a report this evening when I stop by to see how you're doing. Now, I've got to go, or I'll be late."

Shay called at lunchtime to check on him.

He growled, "I'm fine and I'm going to get you for this. Ms. Gladys is killing me with kindness. Come save me."

She couldn't help but laugh.

As soon as she locked up the clinic she headed to Matt's. Her heart beat faster as she drove closer to his house, yet her mind pushed down the excitement. She had no business getting involved with a man who wouldn't be around after the next two weeks.

When she arrived at Matt's house, Ms. Gladys met her in the drive with her mouth pinched with worry.

"How's the patient doing?" Shay climbed out of the car.

The older woman placed her hands on her hips. "He told me he was going to take a nap and locked me out."

Shay put her arm around Ms. Gladys's shoulders and gave her a gentle squeeze. "I appreciate your help today. I know Matt will tell you he's thankful when he's feeling better. I'll check on him, but he should be able to take care of himself from here on out. I'll call you if we need you."

"Please do, dear. His legs really are a mess." Ms. Gladys shook her head and started toward her house.

The lawnmower still sat in the yard and Shay went after it, pulling it in under the carport. She knocked on the door and waited patiently. On his bad legs it would take Matt a while to get to the door, plus she had no doubt he was hiding out from Ms. Gladys.

Finally, she saw the curtain move and an eye peeking out. The click of the door soon followed. It was quickly opened.

"Get in here," Matt snapped, looking around frantically. "Hurry."

Shay stepped inside the house, barely controlling her laughter. "Aren't you being a little dramatic?"

Matt glared at her. "You aren't the one she threatened to bathe!"

Shay burst into laughter. She held her waist as tears rolled down her face. Matt gave her a look of disgust and hobbled off. Working to get the merriment under control, she followed him into the living room.

He plopped into the recliner and pulled the footrest up. His legs looked awful. Soon they would start to itch without mercy. He wouldn't like that either.

"You have no idea what I've endured today and now you're laughing at me. Is this your idea of a good bedside manner?"

She couldn't help but huff at that. Which had him glaring at her again. "I'm not at your bedside. I'm making a house call to check on your legs. Do they hurt? It looks like the swelling has gone down."

"It has. I started feeling better this afternoon. The only problem was that I couldn't convince Ms. Gladys of that."

Shay chuckled, covering it with a cough. She glanced around the room. "You know if you'd open some of these curtains and get some sunlight in here it would help your feelings." She stepped toward a window.

"Don't open that. I like watching TV in the dark, plus I'm afraid Ms. Gladys will look in the windows."

She dropped her hand to her side. "Now you're just being silly."

"I know she's just being nice, but I'm not in the mood." He reached down and scratched his leg.

"Don't do that. I brought you some aloe to put on it to keep down the itching." She went to the kitchen where she'd left her bag on the table. Opening it, she pulled out the plastic jar with the green gel and returned to Matt. She handed it to him. "This should help. I also have a couple of allergy pills for you to take. You should be able to return to work on Monday." She took those out of her pocket. "I'll check on you tomorrow."

"You're leaving me?" His disappointed look fed her ego.

"I am. I have a committee meeting tonight."

His mouth turned down. "Thanks for coming by, then. I'll be fine." His attention returned to the sports on TV. "I'll see you at the clinic."

Shay left feeling like she'd done something wrong. Had he been upset with her for not wanting to stay with him? Being around Matt outside the clinic only increased her chances of heartache. She had enough of those for a lifetime.

But she liked him, like no other man in a long time. Matt intrigued her. Kept her on her toes. Excited her. All of that had been missing in her life. She felt invigorated being around him. She'd been going through the motions, the same old actions, for so long it was liberating to break out of the mold.

By the time Saturday afternoon rolled around, Matt had had enough of being the invalid. His legs were much better but looked awful. He would recover. Having become desperate for company, he answered the door when Ms. Gladys had come over to see how he was. She'd brought him lunch. He'd had mercy on her and been civil, but the person he really wanted to see was Shay.

He picked up his phone and called her. She answered on the second ring. "Matt, are you all right?"

"My legs are fine, but I'm bored out of my mind. If I order in pizza will you join me? Stay and watch some TV. I promise to behave

myself. Just a friendly night in." She took so long to answer he feared she wouldn't do so.

"Sorry. I already have plans."

Disappointment washed through him. "Okay, I understand. See you later." He prepared to hang up.

"Matt?"

"Yeah?"

She hesitated a moment. "If you want to go with me you can."

His blood quickened. "I'll be ready when you get here."

"You don't even know where we're going." Surprise filled her voice.

Desperate to get out of the house, and a chance to see Shay, it didn't matter where they were going. "I don't care. I just need to get out."

"All right. Dress casual and bring a change of clothes."

"Now, that does sound interesting." Where could they be going?

"Don't get any ideas. I can change my mind," Shay said.

"I promise to be a gentleman."

"I'll be there in fifteen minutes."

"Don't bother coming to the door. I'll watching for you."

Shay chuckled. "You really are wanting to get out."

"And I'm looking forward to seeing you." He was, too much.

"Matt." Her voice held a warning.

"Understood. See you in a few." He ended the call.

Good as her word she pulled into his drive minutes later. He was out the door before she stopped the car. He glanced over to see if Ms. Gladys stood at the window. He didn't see her. Opening the passenger door, he threw his bag in the back seat and climbed in. It was one thing to have his neighbor concerned about him, another to have her in his business all the time. "Let's go before Ms. Gladys comes out and starts asking questions."

"In a hurry?" Shay grinned as she backed out of the drive.

As she left the city limits, he asked. "Where're we going?"

"To my farm."

"I didn't know you had a farm."

"I don't talk about it much. It's my hideaway. The one place where I can be me."

He looked at her. "Be you?"

"Yeah. Not the doctor. Not the daughter. Not the daughter-in-law, not a hero's wife. Just plain old me."

"I didn't know you minded being all those things." He'd thought Shay was happy being all things to the town.

Her mouth thinned. "I don't mind most days, but others it's a burden. So sometimes I need to get away."

"You still haven't really answered to where."

She turned and headed out of town going west, putting the sun in their eyes. "We're going out to my grandparents' homestead. I bought it from my parents a few years ago."

"Your mother's or father's side?" As they left the regular stores and businesses of the city and the homes of the suburbs the scenery turned into flat farmland with rows of cotton and corn. Occasionally there would be fenced-in fields with cows grazing.

"It belonged to my grandparents on my mother's side. She inherited it. There isn't much to it, but it's mine. I've spent any extra time I have fixing it up. I had a few things I wanted to do this weekend and you happened to call as I was going out the door."

"How far away is it?"

"About forty-five miles from your place. A little closer from mine."

"You ever thought about moving out there?" He looked out at the rich delta dirt.

"About every day."

He glanced at her. "Then why don't you?"

She pulled up the corner of her mouth. "I don't know. I guess because it's easier to stay where I am."

"Really? Forever? So when you remarry you'll want to live where you and your ex-husband lived?"

She shrugged. "I've never really given it any thought."

"Which one? Remarrying or where you would live."

"Either."

Matt looked at her in complete disbelief. "As smart, vivacious and beautiful as you are you don't think someone would want to marry you? You'd be a real catch. Perfect, in fact."

Shay narrowed her eyes. "Are you offering?"

He gulped. It had sounded like that. "No, I uh…was just saying. Maybe we should change the subject."

"You know I was kidding you about the offer of marriage."

This wasn't what he wanted between them. He'd gone too far. "I'm sorry, Shay. I said more than I should. It's not my business. I should use my manners. I'm your guest on this trip."

Her body relaxed. She made a right turn down a dirt road. Dust billowed up behind them as they traveled. Soon they drove into an area with fenced grass fields on either side of the road. She made a turn up a drive with grass down the center of the lane.

"This belongs to me." Shay waved a hand at both sides of the drive.

"How many acres do you have?" Matt watched as they approached an area with trees. Among them he could just make out the corner of a white clapboard building with a red tin roof.

"There's twenty acres left, but I did manage to save some along the river. Even though it's at the back of the property. The house couldn't be too close to the river because it might flood."

As they drew closer, he could tell the trees were a cluster of large oaks. Shay drove onto a grassy area then around one of the trees and pulled to a stop in front of the house. A porch ran the length of the front. On either side of the door were a set of red rockers with yellow pillows in them. Between the chairs sat a white table with a red flowering plant on it. Everything about the place looked like peace and tranquility. It couldn't be more different from the house Shay had shared with her husband or his apartment in LA.

"I know it's not much, but it's mine." Pride filled her voice.

"I like it. It looks like you."

Shay smiled, obviously pleased with the idea. She had the best smile. It reached her eyes, made her face glow.

"Come inside. I'll give you the grand tour of all four of the rooms."

He followed her onto the porch and held the screen door while she unlocked the wooden door with a glass panel across the top. She pushed it wide and they stepped inside. The walls of the room were painted white and the wooden floor gleamed. An overstuffed sofa sat at an angle in the far corner. Two matching chairs faced a fireplace with a large footstool in front of them. A small desk and bookcase had been positioned against another wall. Thin white curtains hung on each side of the two windows in the room.

"Obviously the living room." She moved to a doorway off the living room. "This is your bedroom."

A regular-size bed with a high wooden headboard and matching footboard filled the small space. A bedside table and a chest of drawers were the only other furniture. A braided rug lay on the same type of flooring as the living room.

She directed him down a short hall to a room to the left. It was a kitchen which looked to have been recently redone in a retro look. Even the refrigerator was a sea foam green. A farmhouse sink faced one of the windows. The small wooden table had two mismatched chairs.

"My bedroom is across the way." She pointed to a door but didn't stop. "The bath is back here."

It was a small room with all the basics. The large two-person claw-foot tub was the showpiece of the room. What he wouldn't give to share that with her. *Stop those thoughts. You made a promise.* "Nice tub."

"Yep. The shower is out back." She remarked it as if she knew exactly what he'd been thinking and wanted to remind him of his place.

"Got ya. You said you had a few things to do. How can I help?" He moved to a window to look out. There were two outbuildings behind the house.

"I didn't bring you out here to put you to work." She fussed with a towel near the sink.

He met her gaze. "Why did you bring me?"

She shrugged. "You sounded desperate to get out and I happened to be coming here. I thought you could rest and see something different than the four walls of your living room. It's also a good idea for someone to keep an eye on you for another day and make sure you've fully recovered."

Matt put his hands in his back pockets and gave her a quizzical look. "Are you sure those are your only reasons?"

Shay turned away. "Yes, that's it. You don't believe me?"

Matt grinned. He made her nervous. She wasn't as unaffected by him as she acted yet she made sure she held him at arm's length. "Unfortunately, I do. Now tell me what you want done."

Shay looked as if she wanted to say more, but she didn't. "I need the yard mowed."

He winced and looked down at his legs. "I'll take care of it with my new knowledge in hand. I know how to stay out of the ants' way now. Where's the mower?"

"It's in the smokehouse. The larger building out back." She pointed out the back door. "If your legs start bothering you, stop."

"Yes, Doctor."

Matt had the yard half-finished when he pulled off his shirt and wiped his face with it, then slung it over the wooden fence. He had made a few passes around the yard and he'd looked over to see Shay outside beside the window she'd been repairing. Instead of working on it she stood with a screwdriver in hand watching him. He waved and she quickly turned away.

Exactly why had Shay brought him here? He wasn't her type. She wanted hearth and home while he was all about ambition and work. How could they ever find common ground?

Shay gulped. Matt had removed his shirt. She couldn't help but stare. The last time she acted this muddleheaded about a man with a bare sweaty chest she'd been a teen. Actually, it hadn't been this bad when she'd been high school crazy about her eventual husband. Where Matt was concerned, she'd lost her sense of perspective.

He smiled at her on his next round.

She pursed her lips and turned her attention to the window. The worst part was that he recognized her desire. After giving him time to make a turn so his back was to her, she looked at him again. He stayed fit. That she would give him. Shay went back to scraping the window seal. With little enthusiasm, she planned to paint before he turned to come back her way. She refused to be caught ogling him.

By the time he had finished cutting the grass, she had gone inside to prepare their evening meal. At the slam of the car door, she guessed Matt had gone after his bag. Not long after the shower started running. That only added to her agitated nerves. The thought of naked Matt standing under the water had her hands shaking.

Subconsciously, had she had an ulterior motive for bringing Matt to her hideout? Was she that desperate? How pitiful. Especially after she'd told him to keep his distance. Why couldn't she just admit she was attracted to him? That she'd liked having his attention even for a little while.

"Hey."

She jumped at the sound of Matt's voice. Had what she'd been thinking been written all over her face? He'd changed into a T-shirt and jeans, but his feet remained bare. His hair stood out, messy and damp. Sexy would be how she'd describe him, if asked. "Hi."

"What're you up to?"

"I'm preparing our supper." She held a bowl in her hand.

He leaned against the door casing as if

he hadn't a care in the world. Like he spent every weekend at a woman's home. "You've done enough for me already. I should take you out to dinner."

"No way. Coming out here is about getting away." She forced her hands not to tremble.

"Okay. I can live with the rules." He stepped farther into the kitchen.

"I thought if you didn't mind, we'd have a picnic. The weather's great." She pulled the large hamper off a shelf and placed it on the table.

"That sounds nice. What can I do to help?" He came close enough she could smell the soap she'd left in the shower rack. He wore it well.

"We need a quilt. There's one in the bottom drawer of the chest in your room. If you would get it." She put the bowl on the counter. It rattled to a stop.

"I'm on it. By the way, I brought your bag in and set it by your door."

"Thanks." As he left she called after him, "You might want to bring a jacket or sweatshirt if you have one."

By the time Matt returned, she had the hamper and small cooler ready to go. He'd put on tennis shoes and had a sweatshirt in hand. "What do I need to carry?"

"If you can get the cooler off the counter, I think we'll be ready." She picked up the hamper.

"Where're we having this picnic?"

"There's a nice spot down by the river. While we're there I need to check on a dying tree my neighbor told me about."

"Dying tree? I've never had to check on one of those before. Shay, you do have fascinating ways of entertaining a man." His heated gaze locked with hers.

Her heart pumped faster. "Come on, we need to load the four-wheeler. It's in the shed."

"Now that sounds like fun."

"Have you ever ridden on one?" She led him to a small shed and unlocked it.

"Nope. But I've always wanted to."

She set the hamper on the ground beside Matt's feet. "I'll back out then we can load the food."

When she had the four-wheeler out, they strapped the containers on a rack behind the seat. Shay climbed on and Matt got on behind her. She put the machine in gear, and they headed down a path she used to the river. She hadn't anticipated how intimate it would be to ride with Matt's thighs pressed against hers or his hands at her waist.

A couple of times she stopped for large limbs that had fallen in the path. Matt quickly climbed off and removed them. The nicest thing about him was that she didn't have to ask him to help. He knew what needed doing and did it. She'd forgotten what it was like to have someone as a partner.

He asked close to her ear so he could be heard over the motor, "Are all these trees yours?"

"They are. They were so close to the river they weren't cleared for farming land. I'm lucky to have them. Most landowners don't have any. Over the years the river has changed course."

"They're amazing."

"They're one of the reasons I love this place so much." She continued driving over the pine needle bed and down into a dry creek and out again. She slowed as she came to a stand of trees. Stopping, she turned off the four-wheeler.

"This is where the tree is supposed to be." She looked up, studying the tops.

Matt came to stand beside her. "What're we looking for?"

"Some indication the tree is dying. See the top of the tree is turning brown." She walked to the tree.

He followed.

She pointed to a mass of sap running out of the tree. "This shows where the bugs have been boring into the wood."

Matt reached as if to touch it. Shay caught his arm, stopping him. "You don't want to get sap on your hands. You'd have a devil of a time getting it off."

"What's the big deal about bugs in one tree?"

"The bugs will spread. In no time they would kill a number of these trees. I'll have to have this one removed and spray the others. These trees have been around too long to lose them now."

"I've never thought about trees or tree-eating bugs." He put his hands in his pockets and looked up.

"I don't guess there's a big call for concern about either in Chicago."

He continued to look at the tree. "There isn't. But who knows, one day that might change and now I know what to look for. Once again, I've learned something from you. Knowledge is always a good thing."

Shay smiled and continued walking as she studied the trees. "I've learned a few things from you too."

"That would be?"

"That I need to stop and listen when someone offers learned help. That there are people who are willing stand up for what's right even if it may hurt them." She grinned at him. "That Uncle Henry has good taste in friends.

"What I don't know is why you don't talk about your family. I've not heard you say anything about your stepfather. What's the deal there?"

By the look on Matt's face, she may have ruined the entire day. His jaw tightened and his lips thinned.

She touched his arm. "Hey, you don't have to talk about him if you don't want to."

"It's no problem." He shrugged. "My stepfather is a man with a well-defined list of what life should consist of. He believes in doing the right thing. That we have to protect those who can't take care of themselves. We should always be the best at what we do."

"He sounds like a good man."

"Yeah, I just wished I recognized that sooner. It took me growing up to understand him better. By then there was such a distance between us I don't know if we will ever find common ground now."

"It's never too late to try." Shay's soft suggestion held hope.

"Maybe so. But I been so busy since I left home and seen so little of them I feel more like a stranger than a family member."

"I can't imagine that ever happening with my family. But everyone makes time for what they want to do."

Matt winced. "I guess I'm just making weak excuses for being a jerk."

Shay touched his arm again. She didn't want him to think she was criticizing him. "I didn't mean to make you feel bad. I know your work takes dedication, but family and our friends are important as well."

He continued to look at the trees for a moment before he said, "Are you ready to go? I want to see the river."

They climbed back on the four-wheeler.

Shay understood Matt better. He'd seen his family so rarely in the last few years that he feared he didn't fit in anymore. She hated that for him. His family must miss him. He needed them and didn't realize it.

CHAPTER EIGHT

Matt watched with interest as they continued down the path. They broke out into open
land on a bluff with the river beyond. He
made an effort not to think about what he'd
revealed about himself to Shay. How he'd
treated his family. They all deserved better.
How had he convinced himself it was a good
idea to stay away? Because of his hang-ups
he had hurt them. That only made matters
worse.

He climbed off the four-wheeler, then
helped Shay off. They stood looking out over
the river with its steady current flowing to
the south.

"Damn, this is amazing. I know the Mississippi is a huge river just from the few times
I've driven over it, but this is unbelievable."

"It's impressive, isn't? Wait until you see
it against the sunset." She nudged him with
an elbow.

"And this spot," Matt said with awe as he looked around them.

"Yeah, it's my special place." And she'd chosen to share it with him. He felt honored.

"You brought me to your special place, huh?" He didn't look at her, instead letting his voice let her know what that meant to him.

"Hey, don't let your head get too big. I had planned this trip before I let you tag along."

"Okay, you have now put me in my place."

"It wasn't intentional. This spot always calms me. Makes me feel better. After John died, I spent a lot of time here. I wanted to have our wedding ceremony here. Just John and me, our families, but it wasn't large enough for John, and the town wouldn't have been happy if they weren't invited."

"You had the wedding that he wanted." It was like the relationship had swallowed her up and taken her over. Where had the Shay he knew been then?

"Yeah. I guess I did."

"Not to speak ill of the dead, but he sounds like he was a pretty self-centered guy."

"I didn't realize that then, but I can see it now." It sounded as if she had just figured that out.

"Have you ever wanted to marry?"

"I thought I did. I had a girlfriend and even asked her to marry me but she turned me down."

Shay turned to face him, sympathy on her face. "Why did she do that?" Her eyes widened. "Forget I asked that. It's not my business."

Matt hesitated a moment. Did he even understand enough about the why to answer? "I'm not proud to admit it, but I guess I was selfish too. I thought she was the one. We were both into our careers. When I realized I had to move I asked her to go with me. I hadn't thought how doing so would affect her career. She said no. I didn't think I could stay. I guess I didn't care enough about her to stay. It's taken me a while to figure that out."

"That still had to have hurt when she said no."

He shrugged. "It did, but I know now that it wasn't meant to be."

"I can't say that the way John treated me doesn't still hurt. We spent too many years together. What I will say is that I learned to be happy with myself, but it took a long time."

Matt winced. Could he say the same about himself? He'd messed up his relationship with Jenna, expecting her to give up everything for him. Then there was his job situation. Could he have handled it differently to preserve his position? And his family? They deserved better than his avoidance. How had his life become such a twisted rope of *wish I had, could I have and can I.*

He couldn't deny that it all hurt. Matt put his arm around Shay's shoulders and gave her a quick hug. "Enough of all that. Tell me what you know about the river."

"Are you sure you want more of me expounding on history and stuff? Haven't you had enough of that?"

"I can never get enough." He took her hand. "Expound away."

Shay cleared her voice as if she were about to present the knowledge of life. "It's the lifeline around here. The Mississippi is the second largest river in North America. The Native Americans called it the Great River. It flows into the Gulf of Mexico. I've heard you can step over it where it begins. I'd like to do that sometime. I can't imagine that since it's so wide down here. Oh, there are only five bridges across it. The main ones are at St. Louis, Memphis and New Orleans. Which means you have to drive a long way around to get to the other side depending on where you want to go."

Matt chuckled. "I certainly hit on the right subject."

She gave him a mortified look. "I told you."

"Hey." He waited until she looked at him. "I liked hearing all of that. I found it interesting."

He stood behind her and put his arms around her waist, holding her securely. His cheek rested against the side of Shay's head. She leaned back against him. They stood like that for a long time. Somehow being with Shay eased his burdens. It had felt good to share his pain over his family. To have her know all of him. The good and the bad.

At his stomach's rumble, Shay giggled. "Let's have dinner before your stomach complains more."

They unloaded the four-wheeler and laid out their meal. Each took a side of the blanket with the food between them. Shay served their plates.

When they were done Shay said, "I bet you think we don't have bright lights like you do in the big city, but I'm going to show you different."

His blood ticked up a notch. "That sounds interesting. What do you have in mind?"

"Help me clean up this food and I'll show you." A hint of humor filled her voice.

A few minutes later they had everything packed away and secured on the four-wheeler.

Shay returned to the quilt and sat down. She patted a spot beside her. "Hurry. You don't want to miss it."

Matt sat close, but not touching her.

"Now watch." She pointed to the west where the sun hung low on the horizon.

He took her hand as they watched the bright yellow sun, then the burst of light turning orange and pink as it fanned out and slowly slipped beneath the land. "That was amazing. You win on the best light show."

"Hey, we're not done yet. The next show is coming up." She pointed toward the river. A barge with lights burning slowly moved up the river. A few minutes later another came by going the other direction.

They watched in silence for a while.

"It's so peaceful and calm here that it makes me not fear anything for just a little while." Her voice was but a whisper, as if she spoke as much to herself as to him.

"What do you fear?"

She sighed. "Sometimes I worry that I'll end up like Delta Dawn in the song. Wandering around town thinking about what was and not living in the 'what is.'"

He wanted to take her in his arms and tell her that wouldn't happen to her. But how could he say that? He wouldn't be around to help make it any different for her. He didn't want to hurt her. She'd had more of that than she deserved. Shay needed someone who would give her security and the assurance that she was the center of his world. He couldn't even bring himself to see his family. He was in the middle of seeing where his life would go, and he had no right to involve Shay in the mess it had become. He wasn't in any position to make promises.

"How about you? What do you fear?"

"That I'll never have another night like this."

Shay watched him for a moment, then leaned toward him and cupped his cheek. "That was the nicest thing that has been said to me in a long time and I needed that." Her lips touched his.

They were as sweet and plump as he remembered. And he wanted more.

Shay's arms wrapped around his waist as she moved closer, her soft body pressing against his. His heart went into overdrive as his blood heated. She felt so good against him. She opened her mouth to him. Matt invaded, taking and giving. Shay returned the need.

Thunder rolled and Shay pulled back. "We've got to go. She jumped up and Matt followed.

"It looks like we're going to get a third light show that I hadn't planned on. This time of the year the thunderstorms can be dangerous. We especially don't want to be in the trees when it comes over us. It can get scary out here quickly."

Fighting his disappointment, Matt grabbed up the blanket into a wad and took her hand. "Then let's move."

Soon they were making the return trip to the house. They had made it out of the trees when the first drop of rain hit him. The wind bellowed against them and a couple of times Shay had to work to keep the four-wheeler steady. The lightning flashed with too much frequency and too close for his taste. He leaned over Shay in an effort to protect her from the pelting rain. With great relief, she pulled up under the shed.

"Leave this stuff." She indicated the items strapped to the back of the four-wheeler. "We'll get it in the morning. Run for the front porch. That'll be easier than trying to go in the back. We can take off some of these wet clothes before we go in the house."

Hand in hand they raced across the yard. Lightning flashed again and Matt saw a smile on Shay's face. Now that they had made it to safety, she was enjoying the experience. When they got to the end of the porch, he picked her up and placed her on her feet under the roof into the dry then he stepped up beside her. Shay had left a light on beside the door.

"This is some weather. Not here one minute and then on top of you the next."

She shrugged. "I warned you."

He grinned. "That you did."

Shay pulled off her shoes and windbreaker. "Turn around."

"Why?"

Her hands went to the hem of her shirt. She gave him a challenging look. "Because I'm going to take off these wet clothes before I go into the house and get us towels."

"You do know I'm a doctor, don't you? I've seen bodies in underwear before."

Her look didn't change. "That may be so, but you've not seen mine."

"Not because I don't want to."

Her eyes widened.

"I'm sorry. I shouldn't have said that." He

shouldn't be thinking it either. Hadn't he already decided that he wasn't what Shay needed in her life? That they were traveling down two different roads? He should be keeping his distance instead of making suggestive remarks. Kissing her. "I'll be a gentleman and turn around."

He waited for the door to close before he stripped off his shirt and dropped it with a plop on the wooden boards. How was he going to stay here with Shay and not act on his attraction to her especially after their kiss? While she talked as if she didn't want to get involved with him, she'd brought him to her special place and kissed him. Was she as confused by what she felt as he was?

Shay returned wearing a large T-shirt that covered her to the top of her thighs. He swallowed hard. She'd never looked more amazing or vulnerable. Her focus left his eyes and dropped to his chest.

"Shay?"

"Mmm."

"Can I get a towel?"

"Oh, yeah." She threw him a towel. He used it on his hair.

"When you're done leave the wet stuff out here and we'll see about them tomorrow."

"Is this a new way to get me naked? If it is, I like it."

Shay looked away from him. "No. I just don't want my floors sopping wet. I worked too hard on them to see them ruined." She began toweling her long hair.

"Let me help you." He stepped close behind her, taking the towel from her.

"I can do it."

"I know that, but I'd like to."

Her gaze met his for a moment, then she dipped her head toward him.

Matt gently rubbed the top of her head then started on the ends of her hair, putting sections between the terrycloth and rubbing it together. What was happening to him? He'd never given another woman this type of care. Shay had a way of bringing out the tenderness in him.

"That feels so nice." She moaned and looked at him.

"Shay, don't look at me that way."

"How's that?"

He sighed. "As if I were a man worthy of you."

"Who said you weren't?" She came up on her toes and kissed the corner of his mouth.

"Shay, think about what you're doing. If we take this further, I want you to know I can't make any promises. I don't want to hurt you."

"I'm a big girl. I know the score and what I want. I can take care of myself. Right now, at this minute, I want you."

The towel joined his shirt in a pile. His hands cupped her shoulders as he felt her warm, sure hands at his waistband.

She released the button on his jeans. "I told you these had to come off."

His breath caught. This he hadn't anticipated from Shay, but he sure liked it.

With a deliberate tug, she lowered his zipper. "I can't have a guest who won't mind."

His mouth found hers. Her hands roamed his chest. She shivered. He pulled her against him.

When he broke the kiss, she said, "I want you to make love to me. I need… I just need."

Shay had no idea what had come over her. She'd never acted like this before. That had been one of John's complaints about her: she wasn't aggressive enough. Here with Matt, it hadn't occurred to her he wouldn't welcome her attention. With John it had been all about him. With Matt he gave more than he took. She'd seen him do it in so many ways.

She pushed at his pants, the wet material

making it difficult to get them off. He chuckled. He took a pace back and finished the job, stepping out of his jeans. His length stood tall and proud behind his knit boxers. She could hardly remember the last time she'd been desired so obviously. It was empowering.

Matt brought her against him. She basked in his warmth, her hands circling his waist and kneading his back.

He kissed her forehead. "I need you too."

She took his hand, leading him inside and down the hall to her bedroom.

He stopped in the doorway. "I believe this is the most feminine room I've ever been in."

She'd chosen to do it in a pale blue with plenty of pillows. A quilt made of pastel flowers covered the brass bed, with its high headboard and a footboard. It sat catty-corner to the door, making a statement in the space. A French provincial dresser with a large mirror was stationed against one wall. She'd positioned an overstuffed chair next to a window with a floor lamp behind it. The ruffled curtains in white with a hint of blue dots finished the look.

"This is all me."

Matt stepped around her and looped his arm loosely at her waist. "I like 'the' you.

And I like your bedroom. I like you in your feminine bedroom even better."

"You don't think all this—" she waved a hand around "—will hurt your performance?"

He grinned. "Why don't you let me know what you think in the morning. By the way, the room suits you." His fingers were featherlight as they trailed down her arm. "Soft, sweet and sensual."

She shivered, her nerves alive from Matt's touch. Shay liked that description of herself. For too long she'd had to act strong and resilient. Be what others expected of her.

He teased the hem of her shirt. "I think we should get under the covers where you can be warm."

The storm still raged outside. Rain tapped against the window. The light in the kitchen flickered and went out.

"There went the electricity. Wait here a second." She went to the dresser and opened the top drawer and found the matches she kept there. On the next flash of lightning, she lifted the glass chimney of the oil lamp sitting on top of the dresser. She lit the wick. Light flickered softly around them.

"I'm glad you lit it. I want to see you. To appreciate all of you." He tugged off her shirt then kissed her. As he did, he reached around her and unhooked her bra. His hands brushed the straps down her arms. It fell to the floor between them.

Matt cupped a breast in each of his hands. He lifted them as if testing their weight. "Perfect."

The way he whispered the word with such reverence made her believe it. He kissed the top of one just above the nipple straining for his touch. Moving to the other breast, he placed his warm mouth over the nipple and sucked. She shuddered. Her center clenched. Biting her bottom lip, Shay stopped herself from moaning her pleasure as her fingers fed through his hair.

As his devotion continued, Matt's thumb hooked into the elastic of her panties at her hips. He tugged them down to her knees, then let them drop to the floor. Standing, he held her hand as she stepped out of them. Backing away to arm's length, his gaze started up her body.

Shay moved to cover herself. Matt stopped her, taking her hands. "You are breathtaking. Please let me admire you. Just so amazing in the lamplight." His eyes locked with hers. "You're amazing all the time."

She loved hearing that from him. Over that

past few years, she hadn't felt as if she were amazing in any area of her life. At the clinic she been giving back to the community that had supported her, while knowing the man who had been her life for so long no longer wanted her. Not just that, but had replaced her with another woman. She needed someone to see her. Matt did.

He walked backward toward the bed, bringing her with him. Pushing pillows to the floor, he jerked the quilt back. He turned her around, so she stood with her back to the bed before he picked her up and placed her on it.

As she watched, Matt removed his boxers. He then lay on his side next to her. He propped his head on his hand. His other came to her belly, his finger drawing small circles on her skin. She sucked in air as her core heated.

She reached to touch him. He stopped her. "No, stay still. Just feel. I want to enjoy you. We have all night."

Shay wasn't sure she could remain immobile. Her body tingled all over. Her blood roared through her veins to her center, creating a throbbing pool. Matt asked the impossible.

His fingers left a hot then cold trail as they traveled up to her breasts. He brushed a finger over her nipple. Her middle contracted. She squirmed.

"You liked that." Pure satisfaction hung in his voice. He gave her other breast the same caress before he leaned over and took it into his mouth.

She moaned, her hips flexing. She reached for him.

"Not yet." He placed her hand on the bed again then returned to loving her breasts. His tongue twisted and tugged. Her breasts went heavy with need. She closed her eyes, soaking in the sublime sensations flooding her body.

Matt's hand continued to work its magic as his mouth left a path of sweet nips along her neck. Her hands fisted in the sheet. Not soon enough for her, his mouth claimed her in a feverish kiss making her think of nothing but him. The need built like the storm outside into something out of control.

His hand left her breasts and skimmed down her ribs, across the plain of her stomach, and brushed her curls before cupping her between the legs. He didn't have to ask her to open for him. She had moved well past the point of no return. The want had taken over her mind. She wanted...had to have him now.

Matt's finger slipped into her ready center. She lifted her hips to meet the push and pull of his hand. Nerves at a heightened pitch tumbled over each other and grew, curled into themselves until she exploded with the fury, and experienced honeyed pleasure.

Matt continued to kiss her as if she were the most precious person in his life. He eased away and dropped a kiss on her shoulder.

Shay opened her eyes to find him watching her. A smile curved his gorgeous lips. She cupped his beard-covered cheek, brushing her thumb across his lips. "You've the most beautiful mouth."

He chuckled. "I like yours too. If I leave you for a sec you promise not to move?"

"I couldn't even if I wanted to."

He tapped her on the end of the nose with a fingertip and stood in all his nude glory. His manhood rose straight and thick in front of him. He headed out of the bedroom door giving her an amazing view of his tight butt. Matt was the best specimen of a man she'd ever seen. He soon returned with a foil package.

"Let me do that." She sat up and took the square from him.

As he stood before her, she slowly rolled the protection over him. Finished, she kissed his stomach.

"Shay," he hissed.

She took his hand and tugged him to the bed. He came down over her, his hot body covering hers. His length pressed her entrance.

"Are you sure, Shay?"

She gave him her best seductive smile. "Oh, I'm sure."

Matt, unable to control his craving any longer, slowly entered her. He paused to appreciate the softness and acceptance of Shay. Her heat welcomed him. Nothing had ever felt this good, this right. His mouth found hers as he pulled back, then moved forward again.

Shay clung to him. Her legs wrapped around his hips, pulling him to her. He pumped deeper, faster, harder. She tensed. Her fingers bit into his back.

With control beyond any he could have imagined, he sank into her once more.

Shay shuddered beneath him as she keened above the noise of the storm. "Matt."

With a final thrust, he joined her in a release that shook him to the core. He buried his face in her neck and moved to lie down next to her, weak from pure fulfilment unlike any he'd ever experienced.

As his breathing eased, he reached for

Shay's hand, brought it to his lips and kissed the back of it.

Under control once again, he nudged Shay to him and shifted around in the bed until his head lay on a pillow. He pulled the covers up over them.

She placed her hand in the center of his chest and caressed the patch of hair there. Soon her breathing turned even in sleep.

By the time he woke, the storm had become a steady rain. The side where Shay had been had gone cold. Where was she? If anything, he didn't want her to regret what they had shared. Too many times he'd disappointed others. His mom, his stepfather, Jenna, even the board members in LA. Himself. He didn't want to do it again with Shay. Particularly with Shay.

He climbed out of bed. Cool air washed over him. Looking into the hall, he could see light coming from under the bathroom door. He knocked lightly, then gave the door a gentle push. What he saw took his breath and shook his manhood into instantaneous attention.

A multitude of candles glowed around the room. Shay, with her hair piled on her head, sat in the large footed tub with bubbles surrounding her. Her face looked flushed from the heat but the sparkle in her eyes was all about a woman well loved.

She grinned. "Hey, there. I was wondering when you'd show up. Close the door. You're letting the heat out."

He kicked the door closed and walked toward her. Placing his hands on the rim of the tub, he leaned down and kissed her. She returned it. Standing, he released the towel and let it drop to the floor. "Is there room for one more?"

A teasing glint twinkled in her eyes and she moved her legs to the side. "Only for a very special person."

With a grin, he stepped into the tub, sinking under the warm water as he faced her. His legs went to either side of her hips. She lay her legs across his thighs.

"Hey, you're splashing out the water," Shay protested.

He ran a hand along her calf across her knee and started up her thigh before he came down again. "Is that really what you're worried about?"

She lightly splashed the water in his direction.

"Now who's spilling the water?" He found her foot beneath the water and brought it to his lips and kissed her instep then nipped at her ankle bone. At Shay's quick inhale of breath, he smiled. He had her. Letting her foot go, it slid under the water. Her foot caressed the inside of his thigh. He reached for a breast peeking out of the bubbles, cupping it in his palm.

He grinned at her wickedly. "I'll scrub you if you'll scrub me."

Her lips went pouty and she looked away from him as if not interested. "I washed up before you took over my bath."

"Then you can concentrate on me."

Her gaze met his, holding it as she came to her knees. "I can do that."

Matt grinned as she moved toward him. Apparently, Shay no longer cared about water on her floor.

Her hand rested on his thigh and skimmed up it. "Is there any particular part you'd like me to start with?"

Red-hot desire shot though him. He grabbed her, pulling her along him as his mouth found hers. What had he done to deserve Shay?

CHAPTER NINE

MATT LEFT SHAY sleeping when he slipped out of bed. He pulled the bedroom door closed behind him as he headed to what was supposed to have been his bedroom. Picking up his bag off the floor, he found shorts and a T-shirt and pulled them on. He wouldn't call himself a cook, but he could put together breakfast.

Putting his hands above his head, he stretched. When was the last time he'd felt this good about life, or been so at peace? He couldn't say. Over the years he'd been with his share of women, but none had touched him like Shay. He'd never experienced such depth of caring even with Jenna. As awful as he thought being turned down by her and his work issues were, in an odd way they'd been a blessing. He'd come to Jackson and found Shay.

Yet he'd added another strand to his already-twisted life. He could become dependent on Shay. He'd feared she might want more when he should've been worried about himself. Would Shay consider a real relationship with him? A long-distance one? Why would she? Hadn't she had that with her husband? That had turned out bitterly. Hadn't his past proven he wasn't good with letting people in? Shay wouldn't accept half measures. She'd be nuts to take a chance on him. He sure wouldn't. But if he were different…

What if he slowed down? Realigned his priorities. Faced his insecurities. Could he capture this feeling forever? Maybe deserve Shay and happiness.

Going into the kitchen, he located what he needed to get a meal together. Even being in this simple home with its history gave him a sense of satisfaction, belonging. This world, the pace, was light-years different than his norm. It soothed his disappointments and fears. Just like the Mississippi River he and Shay had picnicked by, his anxieties had eased under the slow flow of living where people cared and showed it. Getting ahead wasn't everything here: people mattered. He would soak this up while he could, then hold on to it as long as he could in the days ahead.

He flipped the frying bacon and put bread

in the toaster, then he sensed he wasn't alone. Turning with spatula in hand, he found Shay dressed in a thin housecoat standing in the doorway watching him. The soft smile she wore punched him in the gut. He was falling for her.

She held her nose up as if sniffing the air. "Hey, I had no idea you cooked. What you have in your kitchen certainly doesn't show that."

He held up the spatula. "I wouldn't make fun of the man fixing your breakfast. He might not share."

"I wasn't making fun. I was just surprised to hear you in here." She walked toward him.

"Did I wake you? I didn't mean to."

"No. I've been awake for a few minutes. It's nice to hear someone else in the house. It's usually too quiet."

"So, what you're saying is I'm being too noisy?"

"Not at all." She stopped just short of touching him. "What I'm telling you is it's nice to wake up knowing *you* are here."

Matt moved the pan off the burner and set the spatula on the counter. He turned back to her and scooped her into his arms, giving her a tender kiss. She had no idea what it meant to him to feel like he was enough just as he was for someone.

Shay clung to him as he slowly let her down to stand on her own feet. Her gaze locked with his. Warm contentment filled her eyes. They stood there for a while just looking at each other. Something had happened between them last night that he couldn't put a name to or maybe didn't want to. Whatever it was would bind him to Shay forever even after he had gone. Suddenly his new job and his life ahead didn't hold the same appeal they previously had.

Yet he'd made a commitment to the hospital in Chicago. There was his career to consider. How could he be the best if he didn't work in a major metropolitan city with a well-respected teaching university hospital affiliated with it. What he'd wanted and dreamed of was elsewhere. Everything but Shay.

Real life couldn't and wouldn't include Shay and mornings like this. That thought shook him. He looked away and stepped out of her arms. "I better get you fed."

Looking perplexed, Shay pulled the belt on her robe tighter as if protecting herself. He hadn't intended to hurt her. He just needed a minute to process his shaky emotions. He smiled. "Want to help?"

Her expression brightened. "Sure."

Together they finished preparing the meal and sat at the table as sunlight streamed in on them. The scene was almost too perfect.

With their food eaten, Shay said, "Leave the dishes. Let's go out to the front porch and drink our coffee. This is the best part of the day."

Matt wasn't sure how she determined that. Any time of the day with her seemed wonderful to him.

For the next half an hour, they rocked and sipped from their mugs. He'd never done something like it before. None of the women he had been interested in would have settled for something so sedate. Hell, he wouldn't have. Shay and her world brought serenity to his.

Shay couldn't be more beautiful. She'd half pinned her hair up on her head. The other half fell down around her face in the most appealing way. She still wore only the robe. One foot she had tucked under her, while with the other she pushed the rocker with her big toe.

"I've been meaning to ask you how your legs were feeling?"

When he didn't say anything, her gaze met his. Her eyes widened slightly in question.

He must have looked like a lovestruck sap. Love? Was that what he felt? His chest tightened. Loving someone would make him vulnerable. Not having Shay's love could crush him. Did she or could she love him? Did she want to? He wouldn't go there. Instead, he'd enjoy what they had here and now and not expect more. If he did, he might be disappointed. For so long he'd felt he didn't measure up. It would destroy him if he disappointed Shay.

"I haven't thought much about them. I've had other things on my mind."

She smirked. "How about thinking about them? Do they itch?"

"After our hot bath I noticed them. The aloe helps."

She stood, took his hand, leading him into the house and to the bedroom that had started out as his. "Come in and lie on the bed so I can give those ankles a good look."

He flopped back on the bed, bringing his legs up so she could see them.

"There doesn't seem to be any more swelling." Shay studied the welts and gently touched a few spots.

"They don't hurt anymore." He waited until her gaze met his.

"You must've had good medical care." Her eyes twinkled.

"Tell me, Doctor, is this the kind of care all your patients receive?"

Shay stepped closer to him and said in a syrupy voice, "Oh, no, you're special."

He took her hand and tugged her down on the bed beside him. "That's good to hear. I'd be upset if it was for anyone else but me." He lightly brushed her breast and was rewarded with a catch in her breathing. "I'm thinking I might need more special attention."

Shay giggled. It sounded sweet, like a breeze through a wind chime. Despite what life had handed her she still looked forward to the possibilities ahead. She hadn't become bitter as he had. He admired that about her.

She smiled that special smile he'd seen her give only him. The peace she created in him settled over him again.

"We could stay here." She brushed her hand up and down his arm. "But I was thinking we could go swimming."

He hadn't seen a pool. The river wouldn't be wise. "Where?"

"In the pond."

"The pond?"

She stood and pulled on his hand. "Sure. Why not?"

"I've never swum in a pond before."

"Then you haven't been hot enough to swim wherever you can."

He grinned suggestively. "Oh, I've been hot enough."

A touch of pink rose in her cheeks. "You say things like that to get a reaction out of me."

Matt shrugged. "Maybe so but the reward is getting to see how cute you look when I tease you."

She gave him a quick kiss. "Let's go for that swim. It's almost noon and plenty warm enough." Shay popped off the bed.

"I didn't bring my suit," he called as she left the room.

"Who needs a suit?" She let the screen door slam.

Matt laughed. *Yeah, who needs a suit?*

Shay wasn't sure what had gotten into her. She had never been known as a free spirit. The idea of going skinny dipping, especially with a man in broad daylight, had gone way beyond her usual comfort zone. But it had felt so good. Liberating. How long had she lived under the expectations of others? Or those she put on herself? Far too long.

To make matters worse she'd had sex

under the sun beside the pond. She'd taken all that repressed sexual desire and let it out into the world as if it were confetti. Now she stretched across her bed. Matt lay sleeping on his stomach next to her. They'd returned to the house and had a simple lunch and decided on a nap. That had turned into slow, sensuous and spine-tingling sex before sleep took them.

She would have never imagined how much her life would have changed in just a few weeks. It was as if she'd been a firefly captured in a jar, blinking and living, a part of a group of other captured fireflies, then along came Matt, who opened the top and let her out into the world again. She wouldn't be going back into that jar.

Brushing her hand over Matt's back, she watched as the one eye she could see opened. "I hate to wake you, but it's getting late. We need to head to Jackson."

Matt moaned. "Do we have to?"

"We do." She kissed his shoulder and climbed out of bed.

An hour later they drove out the drive toward the main road and beyond the bubble of pleasure they'd created for them alone. She'd always had a sense of sadness when she left the farm. This time it was deeper. Her hours there had been perfect. The old house where her grandparents had been happy now held the same memories for her.

Somehow, she'd found herself again. Or maybe found the person she was meant to be. Matt had made her feel special. Not for being the head cheerleader, who became a doctor, who married the town hero, but cherished for the woman inside. Matt had given her a rare gift. One she would forever treasure.

Carrying around the knowledge that John, who she'd believed for most of her life would always be her one and only, then to learn she wasn't enough for him, had colored her entire world. Matt appreciated everything about her. He'd become her lover, but more importantly he was her friend.

He had only a few more weeks with her and she planned to make the most of them because it might be all the time they ever had. They might be from different worlds, yet they had collided and created something wonderful for a time. She intended to snatch every precious second while she could and hold it tight.

Even though her life remained under a microscope, she wouldn't give up Matt while she could have him. If a fling was what she could have then a fling would be what she would accept. There was nothing like the feeling of being desired. It had been so long since she had been, that the idea she was, and by someone as wonderful as Matt, had her dreaming of more. For too long she'd not been held in a man's arms much less kissed into oblivion. To have that now was a heady feeling. One she wasn't willing to give up until she had to.

Matt placed a hand on her shoulder, his fingers sliding under her hair to caress her neck. "Shay, when we get back to town, I'll understand if you want to keep what happened between us quiet. I know things sort of got out of control between us. I never want to hurt you."

Her chest tightened. "Is this your great sex but I'm moving on speech? If it is, save it. I'm a big girl. I can see about my own heart."

His fingers stilled. "Hell, that's not at all what I'm saying. Don't put words in my mouth."

"Then what *are* you trying to say?"

Matt sighed. She held her breath, waiting for him to speak.

"What I'm saying, poorly apparently, is that I care about you and that I want to see you as much and as often as possible until it's time for me to leave. Then I'd like for us to still see each other when we can."

Shay let her breath go. She looked at Matt in the dimming light of the day as her heart flew. "I want that too."

Matt smiled and returned to rubbing her neck.

She looked back at the road, then braked sharply.

Matt's look jerked to the road. Ahead of them a large piece of farm machinery lay half in the ditch at an odd angle with two of its wheels in the air. It was the only bump in the flat, wide field filled with white cotton hanging on the plant.

"Something's wrong." Shay's voice sent a sense of foreboding down his spine.

"How do you know?"

"I don't see anyone. No one would leave a cotton combine resting like that. They're top-heavy especially when full. We need to stop and make sure everything is all right."

She pulled quickly to the shoulder where the exposed underbelly of the machine showed it was still running. They both got out.

She cautiously moved forward, yelling

above the sound of the engine. "Hey, is anybody here?"

Matt started around to the other side. Shay caught his arm. "Careful, this monster is really leaning."

Making a wide circle around the machine beside Shay, he studied the ground around the machine for a body. A large clear door hung open with a corner stuck in the ground.

"Matt," she gasped as she gripped his arm. "There's someone under it. Rick Stokes, is that you?" There was no answer. The machine creaked. She started forward then came to a stop. "If this falls it'll crush us all."

Matt paused a moment to think. The guy needed their help, but they'd be no good to him if they got hurt. "Move the car parallel to it on this side. If it starts down, it'll be supported by the car, leaving us space to get out."

She looked unsure for a moment as she studied the situation but left him without a word. Moments later she pulled her car off the road near where he stood. He directed her into position.

Shay left the headlights on and turned on the emergency lights. Red flashed around them. Seconds later she was out of the car, carrying her medical bag. She hurried to the young man. "Rick?" She went down beside the man.

Matt joined them, reaching inside the cab and finding the key to turn off the machine. With that done, it became eerily quiet.

"Help." The word was but a whisper from the man on the ground.

A whoosh of air came from Shay. "Rick, how long have you been here?"

"I don't know. I wanted to get home before dark."

Matt went down on his knees beside Shay. A least that news was positive. Rick hadn't been there too long. Time would make the difference between saving the man's legs and having to remove them.

"Shay. Help me. My legs are caught."

"I'm right here. Just stay calm and keep talking to us."

Matt moved in closer to her. The ground was damp at Rick's hips. Matt feared his leg had been cut. Too much blood loss could mean the loss of the leg. He said to Shay, "You call 911. You know where we are better than I do. Tell them we need leg braces. Something to lift this machine off him."

Shay started punching numbers on her phone.

"Rick, I'm Dr. Matt Chapman, I'm a friend

of Dr. Lunsford. I promise we won't leave you. I'm going to check your heart rate and pulse." Matt picked up the man's wrist and found the slow but steady movement of blood. He told those numbers to Shay who relayed them to the EMTs. "Tell them to call in Life Flight."

"They'll want to make that call," Shay stated.

Matt's eyes locked with hers. "Trust me. Tell them there isn't time to waste. He needs to get to the closest trauma one hospital in the next hour or lose his legs."

Turning back to the patient he said, "Rick, can you wiggle your toes?"

"No," he groaned.

"Try. Any movement is important to know." Matt worried Rick's blood flow had been cut off too long.

"I can't."

"Okay." Matt patted his shoulder. "More help will be here soon. Hang in there."

"Life Flight is on the way." Shay joined Matt on the ground again with the phone line still open. "And a wrecker."

"Rick, can you tell us what happened?" He had to keep the man aware. They'd need him to tell them what he was feeling when they got him out.

"I decided to drive over the ditch instead of going all the way down the field to the road. I wanted to save time." He took a deep rattling breath.

Matt looked over at Shay's concerned expression. They needed help soon or they might lose Rick. Not just his legs.

"The ditch was deeper than I thought. A tire came off the ground. I got out. Had to see if I could get unstuck. While I was looking at the tire the combine leaned more. I slipped trying to get away. It caught my legs."

Matt looked at his watch for the umpteenth time. *Where was that emergency crew?* All they could do was wait. Precious time was passing. With relief he heard the whine of sirens in the distance. The noise grew louder by the second.

"I hope the wrecker isn't far behind." Shay looked in the direction of the noise.

She'd voiced his fear. Without it there wasn't much they could do.

"I'll go meet them." Shay didn't wait on his response before she crawled out of their protected space.

The noise became deafening, then suddenly stopped. Matt took a moment to retake Rick's vitals. They weren't what they should be, but they were holding steady. That wouldn't continue much longer if they didn't get him out from under the combine.

The EMTs joined him with Shay right behind them.

One of the EMTs said, "What's the situation?"

Matt relayed the necessary information. He moved out of the way and let the paramedics go to work. Soon there was an IV line in Rick's arm.

"Where's that wrecker?" Matt called to no one in particular.

A male voice outside yelled, "It just pulled up."

"As the wrecker pulls the machine off him pressure needs to be applied to his legs as the pressure of the machine is release. Another person needs to pull him out while one more handles the IV. We need the board in here and leg braces."

"Doctor, we can handle this," the paramedic stated in a firm voice.

Matt met his look. "I appreciate your authority but the medical care he receives right away will make a difference whether or not he walks again. I'm an orthopedic surgeon who specializes in that care. Give me a fighting chance to give Ricky his legs back."

The paramedic waited a moment before he

said, "Okay. We'll do it your way. They told me you were some big-time doctor."

The *beep-beep-beep* of the wrecker backing into position on the opposite side of the cotton picker drew their attention.

"Let's get that board in here," the paramedic called.

The backboard was passed through the opening. They worked to position it into place under Rick's head and shoulders.

A man from outside called, "Y'all are going to need to come out here while the picker is being lifted."

"No way," Matt announced. "I'm staying here. Applying pressure is too important. The ground is already damp with blood. Seconds could mean the difference. The car will protect me."

"We aren't willing to take a chance like that," one of the EMTs said.

"I'm not asking you to," Matt snapped.

"I'm staying too."

Matt gave Shay a narrow-eyed look of displeasure, but didn't bother to argue with her. By the look of determination on her face he'd never change her mind. He moved to Rick's head.

Slipping his arms under Rick's shoulders and clasping his hand over his chest, Matt prepared to pull him out. To Shay he said, "Be ready to apply pressure the second you can."

The EMTs hovered outside of the little tunnel created between the picker and the car.

The metal of the machine groaned and rattled then shattered as it was being lifted. It moved only an inch. Finally, the big piece of equipment shifted far enough Matt could pull Rick out. Seconds later Shay applied pressure to the wound on the left leg while Matt settled Rick on the board.

The EMTs quickly joined them.

Matt moved around to Rick's right side and began running his hands over his leg. Rick winced when he touched his upper thigh. It was broken. "Rick, move your feet for me." Matt watched for the slightest movement. Relief washed through him when Rick's right foot relaxed slightly.

"Good," he told Rick. Matt then turned his attention to Shay. She still applied pressure to the other leg.

Shay met his look. "It's a compound fracture."

Matt nodded. "Let's let these guys do what they do best, get him ready to be transported. The leg needs to be cooled down."

"We have the ice packs waiting," one of the EMTs said as he took over for Shay.

"Don't remove his boots. We need them to slow down the swelling," Matt ordered.

Shay backed out of her side of the tunnel, and he did the same out of his. He walked around the car and joined her near the road.

The encouraging sound of the *whop-whop* of the helicopter could be heard in the distance.

"What do you think?" She glanced to where Rick lay.

Matt's lips thinned. "I won't really know until we get to the hospital. He has major injuries."

They both turned as the Life Flight helicopter set down in the middle of the road.

Matt touched her arm briefly. "I need to go talk to these guys. I'll be right back."

Soon the EMTs passed her with Rick secured on the board and ice packs around his legs.

Matt returned to her at a lope. "They have room in the copter for me. I'm going with Rick. I'll let you know how he's doing."

"Okay."

Matt didn't have time to say all he needed to or wanted to. He gave Shay a quick kiss then ran toward the helicopter.

* * *

Pride filled Shay at the work she and Matt had done. The EMTs had commented it had been the most amazing example of heroism they had ever seen. They couldn't get over her and Matt insisting they stay under the machine while the combine had been moved.

She watched as the helicopter lifted off until there was nothing but dim flashing lights and a hum of the engine. The noise of people moving around her and the slamming of doors said she needed to get going.

One of the guys working on the wrecker helped her back out onto the pavement. She headed for the hospital to check on Rick and to give Matt a ride home. By the time she arrived Rick was already in surgery. Matt had been invited into the OR to watch only because he didn't have privileges at the hospital. Shay waited in the doctors' lounge with the understanding a nurse would let Matt know she was there.

When she grew tired of her own company, she went out to the waiting room to look for Rick's parents. She ended up spending the rest of the time sitting with them. Late in the night, the surgeon who had done Rick's surgery with Matt beside him walked out to speak to the parents.

Dr. Roper, the best orthopedic surgeon in the city, introduced Matt. "This is the man that saved Ricky's legs. Without his initial care there wouldn't have been anything for me to work with."

Matt moved over beside her. "Dr. Lunsford was just as involved."

It was nice to have him remember her. John wouldn't have been so inclusive in sharing the limelight.

The surgeon continued. "Ricky will need another surgery that we've planned for the end of the week. I've asked Dr. Chapman to assist me."

She would see if she could find someone to cover for him at the clinic. Ricky needed Matt's skills. His talents were being underused at the clinic. She'd known that from the first week Matt had been there. He should be where he could do the most good.

When Dr. Roper turned to move away, Matt touched her arm. "I'll be right back."

She nodded.

Matt and Dr. Roper stepped to the side and spoke quietly. They shook hands and Matt returned to her. "I'm beat. Let's go home. I'm not used to seeing a case from start to finish. I usually come in at the middle."

"Pace kind of picked up around here, didn't it?" She yawned.

Matt put his arm around her shoulders and pulled her in close for a hug. "I think you are making fun of me."

"Who, me?" She grinned.

Less than half an hour later she pulled into Matt's drive. "I'll see you in the morning."

He didn't immediately get out. It was one of the few times she had seen him looking unsure.

"You know when you have a night like to-night it reminds you that you need to appreciate the time you're given."

"It does." What was he getting at? It wasn't like Matt not to say what he meant.

"I'd like you to stay with me."

"I thought you'd never ask." She opened her car door and pulled her bag out of the back.

After a shared shower, they climbed into bed. Matt pulled her back against his chest and curled around her as if he wanted to protect her. He kissed her temple. Soon his breathing evened.

She followed him into sleep.

CHAPTER TEN

ON WEDNESDAY MORNING, Matt finished up with a patient and stepped out into the clinic hallway.

"Mrs. Dobbs, it was nice to meet you. Be sure to make an appointment with Dr. Lunsford for the week after next. I won't be here."

"Oh, I'll just wait until you are," the middle-aged woman said.

"I'm sorry, I'm moving to Chicago."

She shook her head. "I hate to hear that. It's hard to find a doctor you like. I was hoping you'd be around for a long time."

"I think you'll like Dr. Lunsford. I can personally vouch for her." In more ways than he could say out loud.

"I'll come back and check her out."

Matt watched the woman leave out the front door of the clinic. He'd miss this interaction with patients, but it had been invigorating being back in the OR the other night. He'd not actually gotten to do the surgery, but he'd watched and even offered help when asked. Many surgeons could be territorial, but Dr. Roper had been aware of Matt's skills. It didn't hurt that Dr. Roper had also seen Matt present a paper at a conference and had read a number of articles he'd written.

"I see you've been charming the female patients, Dr. Chapman." Shay came up beside him with a grin on her lips.

He winked at her. "I'm only interested in charming one woman."

"Then you can consider that done." That special smile formed on her lips.

"How's the new guy working out?" Shay had hired the blond doctor, Dr. Kurt Willis.

"I think he'll work just fine. I'm glad he could start today since you'll be gone tomorrow."

"Sorry to have put you in a bind."

She placed a hand on his arm. "You should be in the OR. I'm glad the hospital board gave you privilege. I know you can help Rick."

"Thanks for the vote of confidence." It was nice having someone in his corner and he didn't doubt for a minute Shay supported him.

The new doctor came out of an exam room and looked toward them.

"I better go." Shay headed down to meet Kurt.

Matt moved to the next exam room door. He glanced at Shay. She and Kurt had their heads together, looking at the tablet. His chest tightened. Matt didn't like that scene at all.

He'd already begun to worry about how he'd handle it when he had to say goodbye to Shay. Maybe he would get enough of her soon, but he didn't think so. In fact, with each day and night that passed it was becoming more difficult. He had to continue to remind himself that text, phone calls and airplanes did exist, but it wouldn't be the same as touching her.

Neither of them had discussed what they'd do when the time came. Yet he'd seen Shay looking off with a tightness to her lips and a sadness in her eyes. What had he done? The last thing he wanted to do was hurt Shay. He couldn't even begin to describe how much he'd miss her.

Shay would never agree to leave Lewisville. This was her home, her clinic, the place she was passionate about, her life. He studied her. Her beauty held him. Shay had outside beauty, but she was even more beautiful on the inside. That was what really captured him. He felt honored she'd shared even a small part of her life with him.

The next evening at her house, he slipped into bed beside Shay. She made some changes in her bedroom, putting a bright cover on the bed and adding pillows with large flowers. New curtains lay over a chair ready for hanging. Pride filled him at how she'd embraced making changes. He pulled her into his arms appreciating her warmth and softness.

"Hey," she murmured. "You're later than I thought."

"I wanted to stay until Rick was settled in ICU." He rubbed his cheek against her hair.

"How's he doing?"

"Okay. He'll have a few more surgeries but he shouldn't have but a small limp."

Shay rolled over and huddled into his chest. "Because you're so wonderful."

He chuckled. "I like having a fan club."

She kissed his chest as her hands came up around his neck. "I'm your biggest."

Friday morning Shay stepped into the office to get some papers to give Sheree. Matt was there on the phone. His brows drew together in concentration.

"Yes, yes," he said.

She quietly picked up what she needed and wiggled her fingers at him as she left.

He gave her a weak smile that didn't make it to his eyes and said into the phone, "I should be able to make that work. I need to check on a few things and I'll get back to you. I'm looking forward to it."

As she came down the hall after speaking to Sheree she saw Matt standing in the doorway of the office. His lips formed a line.

Worry filled her. What was going on? "Is everything okay?"

"Can we talk a sec?"

Her heart thumped harder. She didn't think she'd like what he had to say. "Sure."

Shay entered the office and Matt followed, closing the door.

"What's going on, Matt? You're starting to scare me." She stood facing him.

He took her hands. His thumbs rubbed the top of them a little harder than necessary. "It's nothing like that. That phone call was from Chicago. They'd like me to come up as soon as possible. Monday, if I could."

Shay's hands tightened on his. She'd known this day would come, but it shouldn't be this soon. Or hurt this much.

"The situation has changed up there. The

other doctor is leaving a week early and they're backlogged. They need me now."

The note of excitement surrounded by sadness in Matt's voice tugged at her heart. She'd heard it before when he talked about being in the OR with Rick. He missed his job. His skills were wasted at the clinic. "Then you should go."

His brows drew together. "I don't want to leave you in the lurch here at the clinic." His gaze met and held hers. "I don't want to leave you."

"But you have to. I understand that. We knew this day was coming. You should go on. If they need you to come early then that means they can really use you. You have to go."

"At least Kurt is working so you won't even miss me."

Miss him? She'd miss him with every fiber of her being, but she would survive. She'd changed since he'd come into her life. This time she wouldn't get stuck and not move on with her life. Shay fortified herself to say, "Of course you'll be missed, but you have to do what you need to. We'll be fine here. I want you to be happy."

Disappointment filled his eyes as he squeezed her hands. "I'll have to leave in the morning to make the drive. That means it'll mess up our plans to go to the farm."

Shay's chest tightened, making it hard to breathe. She'd get through this. Just like that he would be gone. "I understand. You need to pack. I'll get you some snacks together for the road."

"I was really looking forward to spending the weekend with you. But I should go. I need to get off on the right foot."

She forced a smile. "I agree. It's important to make a good first impression. You're only leaving a week early."

"But I would have spent that week with you. Maybe we can get together for a weekend soon. You could come see me."

That was a nice dream, but she knew in reality that probably wouldn't happen.

"I'm sorry about this. You know this isn't how I would have planned my leaving, don't you?" Concern still filled his eyes.

"Hey, I understand it's life. We just have to deal." She would take what it dished out and meet it. No more hiding for her. Still it hurt to have Matt leaving.

"Then I'll call and tell them I'll be there Monday." He pulled her to him. "I want to take you out to dinner tonight to help make up for messing the weekend up."

"I'd rather us just stay in. I'll cook something easy and we can watch a movie after we get you all packed. Now, we should see some patients so we can get out of here on time this afternoon."

He gave her weak smile. "I won't miss working for such a demanding boss."

The problem was she'd miss everything about him.

That evening Matt settled on the sofa at his place waiting for Shay to join him after their meal. When the word had gotten out that he was leaving, Sheree had arranged an impromptu going-away party during lunch. She ordered in sandwiches along with cake and ice cream. He'd worked in LA six years and not had that type of attention when he had left. This small group of people, even those who rotated in and out, had become his family in such a short while. Shay had worn a smile while everyone laughed and told stories about his first few days in town, but it hadn't reached her eyes. He sensed she was going through the motions.

As excited as he was to work in an OR again, he hated having to leave her.

Shay joined him on the sofa but left some

distance between them. "How did it go with Ms. Gladys?"

He raised his chin with pride. "She said she'd miss me and if I was ever in town, she expected me to come for a visit. She's bringing over an apple pie in the morning for me to take with me."

"You made a real friend."

"I'm pretty sweet on her too. Which comes as a big surprise to me." It had. After he stopped holding back, he appreciated people more.

"People around here can grow on you."

He took her hand, tracing her fingers with the tip of his. "You certainly did on me. Shay—" he waited until she looked at him "—I don't want this to end here. I know it'll be difficult, but I want to see you every chance we get. I'll come down for long weekends, vacations, holidays. I'm not ready to give you up."

A wry smile came to her lips as she looked anywhere but at him.

"What's wrong?"

"I don't know if it's such a good idea to make plans that we may not be able to keep. I've done the long-distance relationship stuff and it didn't go well. Let's just enjoy tonight and what may come without too many promises that might be broken. That way if it works out it'll be great."

"You do know that I'm not your ex-husband."

"I do. It's not just that, it's where we live. The pace of life we live at. What we want. Enough of that. Let's just watch the movie then go to bed."

He pulled her into his lap. Maybe Shay was right. If she was, he wanted to make sure when she thought of him it brought a smile to her face.

"I was thinking about skipping the movie and moving on to the bed." His lips found hers.

She returned his kiss.

He tenderly made love to her, trying to express all his emotions, including his fears. Was he wrong to suggest they might continue a long-distance relationship? Was he thinking more about what he wanted than what Shay needed? He had no plans to offer her forever and if he hung around, she'd never find that person she deserved. It was past time he thought of others' feelings instead of just his.

With Shay, could he be repeating his past mistakes? Jenna had seen their relationship had turned one-sided. Would Shay soon realize that as well? He couldn't have her think of him as Jenna and his family did. It was important Shay remembered him well.

During the night Shay woke him. This time she showered him with attention. It was as if they were both trying to take and hold tight to all they could for the days ahead. He'd wanted to put his imprint on Shay so she would think of him every night. The problem was he feared she'd done the same to him.

He'd made a commitment to the hospital in Chicago. He had to go. For years, he'd studied and worked for an opportunity to join a world-class hospital where he could be a part of advances in medicine. He couldn't give that up. He had skills that needed to be used to help patients. The adrenaline rush was addictive as well. He'd be lying if he didn't admit to enjoying the notoriety. He'd made a commitment he needed to keep.

As the sky lightened, he loved Shay again hard and fast.

They were putting the last load of his things in the car when Ms. Gladys walked over in her housecoat with a pie in her hand. Matt placed it carefully in the car. He hugged the older woman—something he would've never done a few short weeks before. She returned it. He let her go to find her eyes watery. When had someone last cried for him?

Ms. Gladys said, "You take care of yourself." She glanced at Shay. "Remember some things are more important than others. Sometimes you just have to figure that out." With that, she started back to her house.

He and Shay stood there looking at each other. She blinked a number of times, but there were no tears. "I'll be in touch. Call me anytime."

Shay just watched him, saying nothing.

"I better get going." He pulled her into his arms and gave her a gentle kiss.

She clung to him. When he released her, she stepped back, giving him room to get in the car.

Minutes later he drove down the street, fearing he had just left his heart in Shay's hands with no hope of getting it back.

Pulling into her garage, Shay turned off the car and closed the large door before she lay her head on the steering wheel and let all the misery she'd been holding in flow out. Matt was gone.

She knew better than most what that meant. Hadn't she lived this all before?

With no tears left, she headed inside and went through the motions of living. Finally, she gave up. Fully dressed, she crawled under the bedcovers. She pulled Matt's pillow against her, inhaled deeply and moaned.

She'd brought all this sorrow on herself. Hadn't she known better than to get involved with Matt? He'd made it clear from the beginning he'd be leaving in a few weeks. That his destiny was elsewhere. His leaving this morning had only proven that. What had made her think he would stay for her? She shouldn't be acting this way. Yet, here she was wallowing in grief.

She would give herself today to fall apart then she'd move on. Isn't that what she'd learned to do in the last few weeks? That she needed to move on. Not hang on to what had been. If she saw Matt again great, if not she'd have sweet memories. What she wasn't going to do was stop living the life she wanted.

Matt called that evening, but he sounded tired and they hadn't talked long. He called again on Sunday when he'd arrived in Chicago, but he soon ended the call, saying he needed to get ready for the next day. The distancing she'd expected had already started.

Monday morning, she drove into the clinic parking lot after a long, lonely and listless weekend. Matt not being there waiting for her brought more pain, but she refused to let it control her. She had work to do. A clinic to run. People who depended on her.

Matt had gotten past that wall she'd built and made her care for someone again. What she hadn't anticipated was how hard it would be to let him go. Nothing had come close to this pain before.

At Sheree's knock on the back door of the clinic, Shay let her in.

Sheree took one look at Shay and pulled her into a tight hug. "Aw, honey, I wanted you to let yourself go but I didn't want this for you. Still, that man opened you up again. That's a good thing."

Shay backed away from her. "Was I really that bad?"

Sheree nodded. "Yeah, you were that bad. Now, let's go to work and try not to think about how much we all will miss him."

Shay didn't hear from Matt on Monday. She figured that would be the case. He had to have been busy learning his way around the new hospital and meeting people.

Before Matt left, he'd made arrangements for Rick's transport to Chicago. He and Dr. Roper had agreed Rick needed the advanced care University Hospital could provide for his next surgeries. Rick's surgery had been scheduled for Wednesday. Shay used checking on Ricky as an excuse to call Matt.

His phone rang a few times before it went to voicemail. She savored hearing his voice even though it was a recording. The next day Sheree said there was a call waiting for Shay from a doctor. She went to an office to take the call. When Shay answered a woman on the line said, "Hold for Dr. Chapman, please."

Shay's heart fluttered and her palms turned damp just as they always did in anticipation of talking to Matt.

Seconds later he said, "Shay?"

"Yes." The word came out as little more than a squeak. She couldn't believe how nervous she'd become.

"Hey. I'm sorry I didn't call last night. They have me covered up with surgeries. Rick is doing well. He made the flight fine. We're going to try a new procedure designed for people with Rick's injuries. He'll have another surgery next week. We're hoping since this is a new procedure there'll be no charges for the family. We need the practice."

"That's all good to hear." Why did they sound like strangers giving each other reports? "Somebody so young and who makes his living farming needs his legs."

"They're really doing great work here, Shay. People like Rick are walking again."

There was an awkward pause. She wanted to say all the things she'd been thinking and feeling over the last few days, but that wasn't what Matt needed to hear. He was happy. Excited. That was what she wanted most for him. "It sounds like you're where you should be. I know you'll help a lot of people."

"I hate it, but I've got to go. They're paging me. I'll call soon." It was quiet on the line for a moment. "Shay." His voice had lowered, became intimate. "I miss you."

Matt disconnected before Shay had a chance to respond. She spoke into the silence. "Take care of yourself. I love you."

She did. With all her heart.

Over the next two weeks they played phone tag more than spoke to each other. Shay kept busy by redoing her house. She'd hung the curtains in the bedroom. Sacked up the pillows in the living room and donated them to a local charity. She'd even started to remove a wallpaper border in the kitchen to prepare for painting it. Slowly, but surely, she'd started changing her life. She'd taken some suggestion from the garden club about flowers to plant near the front door. The few adjustments she'd made in the house lifted her spirits. Made her feel more in control of her life.

She'd hoped she and Matt could have a long talk on the weekend, but he texted that he'd had an emergency and didn't know when he would have a chance to call. The next weekend she was busy with a community event she'd volunteered to help at and couldn't pick up when he called.

They were already drifting apart, and she didn't know if she could hold on.

Matt had been busier than he'd ever expected. When he'd had a moment free, he'd been dead on his feet and fallen into bed. He hadn't been so tired that he didn't miss having Shay curled up beside him. Somehow, he had to figure out how to get time off to see her. Even the phone calls he'd been so sure would happen between them had been too few. The last had been so terse the fear they could never find their way back to how it had been niggled him. The fast lane he once lived in and thrived on had gone into hyperdrive. This time he didn't care for it, yet didn't know how to get out of it.

Finally, with an afternoon off he took a long hot shower then flopped back on the bed in the hotel that was his temporary home.

He hadn't had time to look for an apartment. He'd get a few hours' sleep then call Shay and have a long overdue conversation. One not interrupted by him being needed elsewhere.

Matt woke to the alarm he'd set on his phone. Eager to talk to Shay he pushed her speed dial number.

"Hello."

Peace washed over him just at the sound of her voice. He'd missed her. Far more than he imagined he would. It had taken the joy out of his new job not having her to come home to.

"Hey, Shay. It's so good to hear your voice."

"Matt."

He loved the way she said his name as if it was the best in the world. "How are you?"

"I'm fine."

He sighed. Where was the easiness that had once been between them? They sounded like strangers. He didn't want that. When he'd been with Jenna they'd gone long amounts of time without seeing each other, but he'd never had this pain in the center of his chest like he had from missing Shay. "I'm sorry I haven't called you. It's been busier here than I dreamed it would be."

"I understand. What you do is important. Demanding. I read the press release about you coming to the hospital up there on the internet. It said you're an up-and-coming star."

He chuckled. The first time he'd done so since leaving Jackson. How pitiful was that? "I think they say that about everyone they hire."

"Don't say that. You're great at what you do. I've seen you in action."

"I love being in the OR again." It was a part of him he couldn't do without. "But I really miss you."

Shay's soft sigh made him want to reach out and touch her. If he only could.

"You sound happy. I'm glad." Her voice had a strength in it he'd not heard before. Was she already creating a life that had nothing to do with him?

"I am except for one thing. You're not here. I need to see you. Will you come see me? I'd love for you to move up here."

There was a long pause before Shay said, "I won't do that."

Matt didn't blame her. He couldn't offer her what she wanted—marriage. He felt for Shay what he hadn't for any other woman, but the last few weeks had proven he wouldn't be good husband material. His devotion to his job overtook everything else. He didn't even have time to call her. More than that he wasn't sure he'd be a good father and she wanted children. His relationship with his family proved what a poor risk he was. What made him think it was a good idea to ask that of Shay? He already knew she would say no before the words were out of his mouth. "I'm sorry. I shouldn't have asked you that. It wasn't fair."

"No, it wasn't." Shay's words were filled with sadness and a touch of anger. "I knew this long-distance stuff wouldn't work."

He hated to admit it, but she was right. He couldn't even find the time to meet her half-way for a weekend together. "Shay—"

"Matt, I'm not going to give up my life, my work at the clinic to move to Chicago to see you whenever you have time for me. I won't do that to myself. I deserve to be the center of some man's life. I've been the extra, on the sidelines showpiece already. Never again. I want more. I deserve more and I won't settle for less."

Matt couldn't blame her. He wished he were there so he could pull her to him and hold her, reassure her that she was all of that to him. But was she? He certainly hadn't treated her that way in the last few weeks. It had been all about him. "You make it sound like what we've shared meant nothing to me.

That's not true. I've felt more with you than I ever have for anyone. Even my family."

"From what I can tell, you shared as little as possible about yourself with your family as you have with me these last few weeks. I think family and friends is everything. You act like yours are just people you have to deal with. I don't want to be another one of those. I'm not surprised you have an issue with commitment since you refuse to work through your problems with your stepfather. You've been running from them too long. You're looking for a place to belong in all the wrong places. Of course, you live for your job. It's easy to have a relationship when the other person is asleep and when they're awake they revere you for saving their life. True relationships require attention and honesty between both persons—with themselves and each other."

He flinched. "You don't know anything about me and my family. What it's like to never feel like you measured up."

"Have you ever thought you might be part of the problem? I know you don't give them, especially your stepfather, a chance now. Did you ever?" she snapped.

Was she right? Anger boiled up in him at the idea she might be. "Like you have a right to say anything about how I handle my life. Look at you. Up until recently you've lived in a house that looked more like your good-for-nothing husband still lived there than you do. You're so involved in the community you haven't taken time to do something for yourself like travel. It's past time for you to make decisions based on what you want—not on what you think looks good to the people around you."

Shay's voice turned tight. "Thanks for that insight into my life. For your information I've made changes, am making them, but you haven't had time to hear about them."

That statement certainly hit him in the gut. This conversation, which he'd believed would be a happy one had taken a horrible turn. How had they gone from what they had shared to slinging accusations at each other? "Shay, I didn't mean—"

"It doesn't matter what you meant. It was going to be over when you left anyway. I should have been strong enough to say it then. We want different things out of life, want to live in different places, value different stuff. We just didn't want to admit it. Thanks for helping out at the clinic and especially with Ricky. It's been nice knowing you, Matt. Bye."

The line went dead as he said, "Shay, listen—"

He'd lost Shay. He felt physically sick. Here he was almost a thousand miles away where he couldn't touch or hold her or try to convince her they could make it work. But could they?

His chest constricted, making it hard to breathe. Maybe Shay was right. Their relationship had been slowly dying, which made it far more painful than a clean break. He wasn't the man Shay needed anyway. She deserved better than him. Shay need someone who would put her first. Always. He couldn't make that promise.

But all that intellectual knowledge didn't make the ache in his chest ease. For once he'd found a woman who accepted him, cared about him, loved him. He liked the feeling. Shay filled the empty hole in him. Loneliness had been so much a part of his life he'd no longer recognized it until Shay had come into it. For once he started to feel as if he were a part of something special, worth fighting for. Now he'd destroyed it.

A few minutes later his phone rang. It had to be Shay. She must be calling him to tell him she'd changed her mind. She'd give them another chance. He jerked the phone off the bedside table. "Shay?"

"Hey, Matt. It's Mom. Who's Shay?"

"Mom." He didn't even try to keep his disappointment out of his voice.

"What's going on? Are you all right?"

How like his mom to care. No matter how he treated her she still loved him. He had treated her badly. She didn't deserve it.

"I'm fine." He sighed. "No, Mom that's not true."

"Tell me. Even if I can't help, I can listen."

Hadn't his mother always listened when he'd given her a chance? When had he stopped giving her that opportunity? Too long ago. "There's this woman I met. Her name is Shay. She's one of the most amazing, selfless, caring, funny people I've ever met. She has this old family farmhouse she's redone. When her community needed a clinic, she'd started one. There's nothing she can't do."

"It sounds like she's a special person. Someone you really care about."

Or someone he loved. "I do care about her. A lot.

"She has her clinic and I have my work here. I don't see how we can make it work." Matt groaned. "And I messed up what we did have. Worse, I'm up here and she's in Jackson."

"Are you not at the clinic in Mississippi any longer?"

"I'm in Chicago. I came up here three weeks ago."

"Matt, why do you insist on keeping us at arm's length? We care about you and want to know where you are and what you're doing. I worry about you." His mother's disappointment and hurt rang clear. She sounded too much like Shay. Had he been treating Shay the same way he'd been treating his mother and the rest of the family all these years? Everything one-sided. And that being *his* side.

"I'm sorry, Mom." He hated always having to say that to her. To feel as if he was failing her. That had to stop.

"All you have to do is open up to us." His mother gave him a moment to let that sink in. "Are you liking your work?"

"I do. I thought this would be a great place to build a career." Why didn't that interest him as much as it used to? Because he feared he'd left the truly important part of his life back in Mississippi.

"But not so much now?" she asked softly and with concern.

"I don't know. What I wanted and what I can have seem to be two different things."

"That's life, son. Sometimes it doesn't go the way we planned. Life has to be about more than work. Having someone you care about and can grow old with matters as well."

"Like with Dad?"

There was a pause before his mother said, "Yeah. But we can change directions and make something different, just as good maybe even better."

Had his mother been as lonely as he when his stepfather, Michael, had come along? Matt had never really thought about how his mother's life had changed when his father had died. Once again, he'd been more focused on his life than hers. That had worked when he was a boy, but as a man he should know better.

"I know you and Michael haven't ever seen eye to eye. I know you've always thought it was his fault, but some of it has been you. It was difficult for you to accept him into what had become our life. By the time Jane and Ben came along, Michael gave up and focused on them. I saw how that hurt you, but you never gave him a real opening. But that doesn't mean he doesn't care about you. You are a part of our family. We all love you."

In the background Matt heard his stepfather ask, "Is that Matt? I'd like to talk to him." A few seconds later Matt's stepfather's gruff voice came on the phone. "Hey, Matt. Your mother told me what happened in LA. I wanted to let you know I'm proud of what you did. That took guts. It was the right thing to do."

Matt swallowed hard. Shock shook him. If his stepfather had ever said anything like that to him before, Matt didn't remember. "Uh...thanks."

"How did the patient do?"

"Great. He has full use of his leg." The strain in Matt's shoulders relaxed.

"All because of you. And come to see us when you can. Here's your mom."

Matt wasn't sure what dimension he'd gone into, but he liked it. He was speechless. Shay had pointed out more than once that his stepfather had set a good example. Matt just didn't want to see that.

His mother continued, "The reason I called is your brother and sister are coming for a visit in a couple of months. I want to get on your calendar. It's been too long since we've all been together. I wondered if you would try to come too?"

Suddenly, he wanted to reconnect. See if

he could find common ground with his stepfather. To do his part. "I can't promise anything for sure right now, but you have my word that I'll really try. I'm not just saying that."

"That's all I can ask for."

Matt didn't miss the note of joy in his mother's voice.

"And Matt...about Shay. You need to think long and hard about what you really want. Think about it. Sometimes we don't get a long time with the ones we love."

"Thanks for loving me even when I've not been very lovable."

"What are mothers for? Others will love you too—you just have to give them a chance. I look forward to seeing you soon. Bye now." His mother hung up.

She'd given him a lot to think about. It was time he started thinking beyond himself. To look at how other people saw and felt about things. Like Shay. He had to decide how he wanted to live his life, and with whom.

He paced across the small room that he was learning to hate.

Was he trying to fill a void with his work that was no longer there because he'd had Shay? Had he been using the adrenaline rush of surgery and long hours to cover his inability to face people he cared about? He did good work, he didn't doubt that, but did medicine fill his need to be needed? While Shay used medicine to care for others.

He stopped to look out the picture window to the busy city far below.

She'd accused him of wanting her to make all the sacrifices. Hadn't he? Was that what he'd wanted from Jenna as well? He'd not treated her with any more respect than he was treating Shay. What did it take for him to learn his lesson? He'd treated his parents the same way. He was an intelligent man who should have seen the pattern before now. He'd been thinking only of himself for so long that he couldn't view life any other way. Until Shay pointed it out. He'd have to work at it, but he'd start acting differently. Figure out some way he could be worthy of Shay.

CHAPTER ELEVEN

OVER THE NEXT two months Shay poured all her efforts into her work, community activities and clubs. If she stayed busy, she wouldn't think about how much she missed Matt. Or how really happy she had been when she had Matt in her life.

She couldn't believe he'd think she'd just pick up and come join him in Chicago. He hadn't even offered her any commitment. Her life was here. At times she'd felt her community had expected something she couldn't give them, but still this was her home. People depended on her. She couldn't just dump it all so that she could be there when Matt had time for her. Didn't he know her better than that?

If she had let him, he wouldn't have treated her any better than John had. Those days were gone. She would have all of him or none. Never again would she be second in the life of the man she loved. Where she couldn't speak up for herself before, she had to with Matt. She wouldn't be an afterthought. She deserved better than that. And would see to it she got it.

Yet, she'd found something with Matt she'd never experienced with John. It made it even harder to lose Matt because he had seen her. The real her.

Everything she did seemed surrounded by memories of Matt. He'd ruined the peace she found going to the farm because all she wanted was him there with her. At her house she started sleeping in the guest bedroom because she didn't want to sleep in the bed they'd shared without him. The joy of working at the clinic had been taken away. Patients came in and asked about him all the time. Each time it happened it was like another reminder of what was gone.

On a Wednesday evening, she pulled up to her parents' house and parked. They had been inviting her to dinner more often. They didn't say it, but she could see in their eyes that they worried about her. She'd lost weight. Sleep came only after many long hours of tossing. Her parents weren't the only ones who had noticed. Sheree, who usually teased

Shay out of a mood, had given that up. Shay got more hugs instead.

"Hello," Shay called as she entered her parents' house through the kitchen door.

The design of the house looked much like hers except it sat in the center of a large farm. A fence surrounded it, creating a spacious yard with a few trees near the house. Shay had always loved her mom's kitchen. So much so she'd patterned much of the farm's kitchen after her mother's.

Shay inhaled the smell of cooking roast beef and potatoes. Her mother had made one of Shay's favorite meals. Matt would like it. Why did everything go back to him?

Her mom stood at the kitchen sink washing fresh fruit.

"Hi, Mom."

"Hi, honey."

Shay put her purse down on the empty chair by the door. The calmness and familiarity of the atmosphere eased her tight nerves.

Her dad came into the room and gave her a hug. "How's my girl doing?"

"I'm all right."

He studied her a moment. "Staying busy at the clinic?"

"Yeah. The new doctor is working out great."

"Is he as good as Matt?"

Her mother cleared her throat, and Shay's father looked at her.

No one was as good as Matt. "Dr. Willis is good. The patients like him."

"Supper is ready," her mother announced almost too brightly.

During the meal their conversation went to the weather, an issue at church and one of the families in town whose son planned to marry. Shay had the sense her parents were talking around what they really wanted to say.

Her father put his fork down on his empty plate and set his napkin on the table before he reached across and touched her arm. "We're worried about you, honey."

This was why Shay had been asked over. Her father wore the same concerned expression he had when what John had done exploded around her. His forehead wrinkled as he watched her.

"We're concerned you're making yourself sick. We love you and want to help," her mother said.

The words hung in the air thick and stifling. Shay couldn't look at her parents. She could hear her heartbeat in her ears. "I'm fine."

Her mother said softly, "I know you really

liked Matt. I saw the way you looked at him. It was so nice to see you start living again. We understood why you threw yourself into starting the clinic, but that wasn't the same as having someone you cared about. The clinic helped you to heal, but Matt made you light up again."

Her father gave her arm a gentle squeeze.

"The clinic is a worthy cause, but it isn't the same as having someone to love and come home to. We know you and Matt were spending a lot of time together before he left," her mother continued.

There was the gossip again, but it didn't bother her. She had liked Matt. In fact, she loved him. That was the problem.

"How can we help you?" her father asked.

"This is something I have to work through myself."

"If two people really care for each other there's always a way to compromise," her mother said softly.

Shay wasn't sure that was true where she and Matt were concerned.

"Do you ever hear from him?" her mother wanted to know.

"I did for a while, but he was super busy, and the calls got fewer and fewer. It wasn't working so I broke it off."

"Honey," her father said. "You need to figure out what'll make you happy. Then figure out how to make that happen. Not worry about what others think you should do."

"I wish it was that easy." She feared what she wanted had already been lost.

"What you lived through with John wasn't easy. But you did it." Her father patted her hand. "Nothing worth having is ever easy."

How like him to speak the truth practically.

He smiled. "Think about it."

Half an hour later Shay drove up in front of her house. Despite the changes she made she didn't want to go in. That part of her life was behind her. Without giving it any further thought she continued on and headed for the farm. It wasn't that much farther to drive to the clinic from there.

She had to pull out of this Matt-induced stupor and take control of her life. Her parents were right. She'd wallowed long enough. Shay refused to continue to live in the land between what could be and what wasn't.

At the farm she sat at the kitchen table with a pad of paper and wrote "Changes to Make" across the top. Sell house. Move to farm. Set up schedule at clinic where she wasn't doing everything. Create a come in early/late schedule for the doctors. Form a fundraising committee for the clinic that she didn't head. Give up all civic clubs except for the garden club. Start going to the small church near the farm. Call Matt and see if she was still invited for a visit.

Shay felt better about herself than she had in years. Now she could start building her future. Hopefully with Matt in it in some way but if not, she'd be living the way she wanted. Not in the way she always had.

Tomorrow she would call the real estate agent about selling the house. On the weekend she would start sorting and moving her belongings. She was determined to start working her list as soon as possible. She had a plan and for once in a long time she liked herself.

Matt pushed the OR doors open. The case had gone well and for that he was grateful, but something still didn't feel right. He wasn't as satisfied with himself as he should be. It had been a tough surgery and he wanted to share his success—with Shay. Yet she wasn't there for him to do so. It was time he faced it. He wanted to be elsewhere.

He missed Jackson and the way of life he had for too short a time. The pace of the place. Looking at the stars. The grandeur of the Mississippi River. The pine trees. The farm. The people.

He pulled off his surgical garb and tossed it in the dirty bin with more force than necessary. The truth was he'd never been lonelier in his life. He missed Shay. His and Shay's conversations over the phone, despite being brief, had eased the frantic pace of his life that living in Chicago had created while they lasted.

He wished for the contentment Shay's simple farm house gave him when he returned to his sterile box hotel room. It had been months and he still hadn't found an apartment. Each one had something that didn't suit him. He huffed. What didn't suit him was Shay not being in them with him.

Was this what he wanted for his life? Did he want to live like this? The demand on his time might slow down, but what would he have then? An apartment someone else had decorated, a great view of a busy city, and no one to share it with.

He walked down the highly polished floor of the hallway toward his office. At one time none of that might have bothered him, but after what he'd experienced in Jackson, he wasn't sure he'd be satisfied anymore. He wanted to sit on a porch and drink coffee while he rocked. Wanted to skinny dip on a hot day. Wanted to eat a homemade apple pie. Most of all he wanted to see Shay smiling at him and to pull her to him for a kiss.

He'd not been pleased with what had led him to Jackson and Shay, but he was grateful for it. Because of what had happened in LA he'd had a chance to experience what his life could be like. He'd unearthed a place where he belonged. Hadn't that been what he'd been searching for? His mother was right. Having someone special in your life was the most important thing. He'd found it, then shoved it away for position and money and lost Shay and the tranquility she brought to his life. With her he had found home.

Would she take him back? If she would, he'd open his heart and feelings to her without reservations. He couldn't correct the mistakes of his past, but he could vow to never knowingly keep her closed off from how he felt—like he'd done with his family or in his other relationships. He would offer her his entire life, his devotion and most of all his fidelity. Shay would be his all. In all things he would consider her first.

He picked up his phone. It was time to accept that he'd made a mistake. He would start correcting it right away.

Matt's nerves were about to get the best of him. He was finally back in Jackson. After giving notice two weeks ago, he'd sold his car and bought a truck and headed south. His boss at University Hospital hadn't been pleased with him, but Matt had given him two names of surgeons who would be glad to fill Matt's empty position. He'd even called them to make sure they would relocate. That had eased the displeasure some.

Shay had phoned, but he'd miss the call. He hadn't returned her call, wanting to talk to her face-to-face. He desperately needed her to see his sincerity on his face, in his eyes. He didn't want her to misconstrue anything he had to say. He could be making a mistake by surprising her, but he'd take his chances.

Matt drove straight to Shay's house when he'd arrived in Lewisville. There was a for sale sign in the yard, and she wasn't home. He saw a neighbor in the yard and asked if they might know where Shay was. The woman said she now lived out at her farm.

He drove toward Shay's farm. While he'd been gone the leaves had turned and there was a nip in the air. Would Shay have a fire burning? The bigger question was would she let him in the house.

Making the turn down the lane to the farmhouse, he took a deep, fortifying breath. His life, his happiness hung in the balance. What happened in the next few minutes could change his world for better or worse. A petite, strong-willed woman held it in her hands. He'd brought this situation on himself and he planned to humbly pay his dues. Whatever he had to do to fix things between them.

With relief, he saw her car parked in front of the porch. He pulled slowly around and up beside it.

Shay stepped out of the house. She wore an oversized sweater, which she pulled tight around her and crossed her arms over her chest. Her hair hung free. Matt winced. Not the most welcoming stance. To his deprived eyes she'd never looked more beautiful. He continued to study her closely. She'd lost weight. Because of him?

Her focus remained on his truck as if trying to figure out if it was familiar or not.

Climbing out, he closed the door and stepped to the front of the vehicle.

The shock on Shay's face made him unsure of his decision to surprise her. He smiled.

She grabbed the top of the closest rocker. "Matt. I hadn't expected to see you."

The sweet sound of his name on her lips filled him with warmth. His smile grew.

"You didn't have to go to this much trouble to return my call."

How like Shay to find the humor in a situation. "I was in the neighborhood."

She looked at the wide-open land for a moment and shook her head. "I don't think so. If you come here, you mean to."

"You got me. I came to see you."

"From Chicago?" Disbelief filled her voice.

"Yes. I need to tell you something." He stuffed his hands in his jean pockets to keep from pulling her into his arms.

"What?" Concern filled her eyes as she tugged her sweater tighter.

"I decided the job in Chicago doesn't work for me."

Her eyes went wide. "Why?"

"Because it isn't what I want anymore."

"You don't?"

"No. I've joined Dr. Roper's practice. We both think it's a good fit. He likes doing the routine stuff and I'll be doing the complicated work."

"You're moving back here?" Shay said the

words slowly as if having a difficult time understanding their meaning.

"Yeah. I have all my worldly belongings right here." He patted the hood of the truck.

"You bought a truck." Wonder surrounded the statement.

"Somehow it's better suited to life here. I may even buy a four-wheeler."

Shay just looked at him in disbelief.

Matt cleared his throat. "Can we talk? Would you invite me in?"

"I guess I can do that. Would you like to come in?" She turned toward the door.

He grinned. "I would like that."

Shay stood in front of the fireplace where a gentle blaze burned.

Matt took one of the chairs. His gaze met hers as he patted the arm of the other chair. "Will you come sit?"

She sat in the chair still looking unsure about what was happening.

Matt turned so he could see her clearly. "I went by the house and saw the for sale sign."

"Yeah. I decided it was time to move on."

"I'm proud of you. Not so much of myself. I've spent too much time thinking about what I thought I wanted without any consideration of others' feelings—especially yours. When I left here I didn't understand that this land, this world, these people were ingrained in you, making you who you are. I didn't grasp what it was like to have those types of connections because I've never had them until you showed me they existed. I became a better person by knowing you. I have discovered where I want to be, to belong. Please tell me you'll forgive me and will give me another chance. If you don't want a future with me, I'll remain your friend. I think Jackson is large enough that we don't have to see each other if we don't want to." Matt took her hand and she allowed it. "But I'd rather you take pity on a misguided surgeon and take him back into your life."

Her face brightened. "I think I can do that."

"Just think? Would it help if I said I love you?"

"That would make it a sure thing." She flung herself into his arms and kissed him.

Matt's heart soared. Shay smelled fresh and healthy. All that he remembered and more, better.

"I love you too," she said against his lips.

Her kiss was honey to a hungry man. "Even though our lives have been driven by different ideas I want us to move forward together."

Shay blinked then blinked again. "You do?"

"Of course, I do."

"That's not what it sounded like during our last conversation."

"I think I was too scared of my feelings to admit them to myself, much less you. I've spent so much of my life pushing people away I didn't know how to let you in. I thought you could never really care for me. That there was too much for us to overcome to have a future. I promise that I'll work to make up for all the pain I caused you over the last few months, even if it takes the rest of my life."

She cupped his cheek and stroked his beard. "You don't have to make up for anything. I needed to make some changes in my life too. You forced me to see that. I've lived too much by what had happened in the past. I needed to be my own person. My parents were worried about me and confronted me about what I wanted out of life. Truthfully, they were worried about me moping over you."

"You moped over me?" He grinned, but it pained him to think about what he'd put her through.

"Hey, don't get too full of yourself."

His arm tightened around her waist. "I'm really sorry I hurt you."

"I needed to hear what you said. I'm selling the house which should have been done years ago. I'm living here where I belong. I've given up clubs and committees I was doing just to be doing. I told the committee wanting to put up a statue to John that they were welcome to it, but that I'd not participate. Believe it or not I've given up some control at the clinic. I was even planning a trip."

"You have been busy."

He grinned as she raised her chin in satisfaction. "I've never felt better in my life. Until now. You were right. I needed to do it. It's like having a weight lifted off me."

"I'm proud of you. You're a brave woman. Where are you going on your trip? Could I maybe come with you?"

Her gaze met his. "I was coming to see you."

"In Chicago?"

She nodded. "I was waiting on you to return my call. I wasn't sure you'd want to see me."

Matt kissed her deeply. "I'll always want to see you. More than that, I want you. That's not exactly right either. What I want is you if you'll have me."

"I'll have you." She whispered into his neck. He kissed her not with the hunger he would've imagined he would have, but with the tenderness of knowing he'd almost lost her. And that it would've been his fault. He poured his feelings into caressing her lips, her cheeks, her eyes, and nibbling at her ears.

Shay returned his affection with enthusiasm.

They broke apart, breathing heavily.

"I have missed you so much." Matt gave her another quick kiss. "But I have something more to tell you. I've made some changes too. I went to see my mom and stepfather on the way down here. It wasn't easy, but it had to be done. My stepfather even said he was proud of what I had done in LA."

"I know that meant the world to you to hear him say it." Shay hugged him.

"It did. I don't know where things will go from here, but I know I've tried. I can't fix years of hurt feelings overnight, but I've made a step forward and it feels good."

"I'm proud of you. That had to have been difficult."

"It was, but worth it. I've only been more scared when I drove down your drive not knowing what reception you'd give me. After having you in my life I understand why my mother married again. Why finding true love is important. Maybe I was responsible for closing my stepfather out, but I'm doing what I can to open that door again."

Shay cupped his face and looked directly into his eyes. "All you can do is try. I'm not worried that he won't recognize what a special man you are, just as I do. Are you sure you'll like living here and working with Dr. Roper? I want you to be happy too."

"I promise I'll be happy here. I want to be here. I think I can build a real and successful career here. Best of all you'll be here beside me."

"I don't want you to regret leaving Chicago for me. Ever."

"Are you trying to get rid of me?"

"No, no, no." She kissed him. "You'd just had your heart set on someplace bigger."

"That's because my heart didn't know what I really wanted and needed. I found myself in Jackson, with you."

"I just want you to know that I'd leave here for you. I wouldn't like it, but I love you more than any place or person."

"That's good to know. But I'm staying right here. Just so you understand, I'm not giving up anything, I'm gaining everything. I had nothing before finding you. You're my present and my future. The past doesn't matter. This is me happy. And in love with you."

She kissed him from the depths of her full heart.

"I do have to leave in a few weeks. I told my mom I'd be at her house when my brother and sister plan to be at home. Will you go with me?"

"Of course, I'll go with you. I'd love to meet your family."

"Great. I think it's a good idea for them to meet you as soon as possible. I don't want them to get to know you for the first time at our wedding."

"You're pretty sure of yourself, Dr. Chapman."

He grinned and kissed her. "I'm not letting you get away."

"I'm glad to hear it. I promise I'm not going anywhere without you."

EPILOGUE

Shay stepped out of the SUV with her father's help. She picked up the front of her wedding dress and let it drop, then fluffed it out. She felt like a princess in the boatneck dress with capped sleeves and a tight bodice that fell into a full skirt. Her mother's pearls encircled her neck.

She looked at the glimmering ring on the finger of her left hand. It sparkled in the late-afternoon light. It had been the one Matt's father had given his mother.

Matt had said, "Now everyone will know you are mine."

Shay liked the idea of being his.

Taking her father's arm, they walked together toward the river. The setting sun had turned the sky to pink and orange. The horizon made a picturesque backdrop to the handsome man with the beautiful smile waiting for her. Dressed in a dark suit, Matt stood at the end of the aisle created by their families, including his stepfather and a handful of their friends. Matt had issued a special invitation to Ms. Gladys, who was providing the apple pies instead of a groom's cake.

Matt stood tall and strong and steady. Shay didn't doubt he would be there for her during the good times and the bad. She'd always know his love and support. He'd already shown her that in so many ways. She could count on him.

Shay would continue her work at the clinic, but with two additional doctors, not just one. Soon she would start the process of expanding. But for now, enjoying time with the man waiting on her would be her focus. They planned to travel to see all the places they had talked about. Their first stop would be Paris for their honeymoon.

They had agreed to live at the farm. When they had children, they'd build a home somewhere on the property, but the farmhouse would remain their private getaway.

Her gaze locked with Matt's. Those green eyes never wavered. She gripped her bouquet of daisies tighter. She would soon be joined with him forever. He would soon be all hers. Not the town's, not the country's, not the world's—but hers.

Shay had never been happier in her life. Her smile broadened as she approached her future. Matt returned it with a twinkle in his eyes. Her father kissed her cheek and left to stand beside her mother.

Matt took Shay's hand. "I love you. When I'm with you I'm home."

"And I love you. Where you are is where I belong."

Together they turned to the preacher.

* * * * *